Small Town Suspicions

Issy Brooke

Text copyright 2015 Issy Brooke

Cover credit: background vector illustration Denis
Demidenko via 123rf.com

Cover design and dog illustration by Issy Brooke

Author's Hello

Just a quick heads-up on the whole spelling and grammar thing. I'm a British author and this book is set in England. Sometimes, British English looks unfamiliar to readers of other variants of English. It's not just spelling (colour and realise and so on) and not just the vocabulary (pavement for sidewalk, mobile for cell phone) but there are differences even in the way we express ourselves. (In the US, it is more common to say something like "did you see Joanne?" whereas in the UK we would say "have you seen Joanne?" and so on.) Also, my characters do not speak grammatically correct sentences - who does? Not me. Rest assured this book has been copyedited and proofread (errors, alas, are my own and I won't shoot my editor if you find any.)

And another thing - locations. Lincolnshire is real. It's a massive rural county in the east of England, with a sparse population. It's mostly agricultural. Upper Glenfield, the town in this tale, is fictional. Lincoln, the main city nearest to Glenfield, does exist and it's worth a visit. The only thing

3

I've fictionalised in Lincoln is the layout and situation of the police station.

You can find out more about Lincolnshire and the characters in Glenfield at my website, http://www.issybrooke.com

Why not sign up to my mailing list? You get advance notice of new releases at a special price - but no spam. No one wants spam. Check it out here: http://issybrooke.com/newsletter/

CHAPTER ONE

Penny May stamped her way along the path, her flapping sandals making an unsatisfying scuffling sound. Her frantic pace and the sultry July heat was doing nothing to take the edge off her frustration.

"She has got to go!" she muttered. A passing teenager looked sideways at her and hunched over, pulling out their mobile phone in case she did anything video-worthy and potentially shareable, and Penny realised that she had been talking aloud. She did it all the time, but she usually had her dog with her, so it didn't matter.

Or if it did, no one was going to dare to question her when she had an excitable Rottweiler bouncing around at the end of her lead.

Francine has got to go, she repeated in her head. *I wish that she were a horrible person. If she stole my teabags or left socks on the floor then I wouldn't feel so bad about telling her to get out of my house. She really has overstayed her welcome. But her niceness creates a force-field around her...*

And now Penny was late for the public meeting about the Sculpture Trail for Upper Glenfield, and she'd walk in and disturb proceedings and everyone would look and some people would sniff and gossip about her because she was still – three months on – that "mad London woman with the nutty dog who keeps finding dead bodies."

The community hall came into view, surrounded by cars. The parking area was full and more vehicles lay scattered along the road, in defiance of the yellow lines prohibiting parking, and in many cases blocking the pavement. The meeting was clearly a popular one. Penny hesitated at the porch, and breathed in deeply.

She wouldn't let Francine's presence spoil her mood. She shouldn't. Francine needed some space and Penny liked the dippy ex-colleague. And the Sculpture Trail was an exciting development for the small town, and she wanted to be involved. She was looking forward to listening to the various artists' proposals, looking at the designs, and debating with the other residents of the town about who should be chosen.

She stepped into the cool entrance hall and saw immediately through the cross-hatched glass of the next set of doors that the meeting had not yet started. The hall was laid out with ranks of wooden chairs, and most of them had been taken, but people were leaning towards one another, twisting around, and chatting. Penny pushed the double doors open and was hit by a wall of conversation. At the far end of the hall, the table on a raised platform was empty, though it was covered in folders and large sheets of paper.

Penny made for the far end, and towards the back, where there were a few empty seats remaining. Some people turned around to see who had just arrived, and she realised that everyone must have been expecting the town council members to enter. In the very middle of the block of seats, a large black beehive wobbled and began to rise up.

"Penny! Now then! Come and sit here, my love! Budge up, Raymond, there's a love."

"Hi Agatha. No, no, it's all right. I'll sit back here." Penny waved and pointed. There was no way was she going to push past all the people who were already seated.

But Agatha was an unstoppable force, like an

elaborately coiffured tsunami. The small, round hairdresser began to plough her way along the rows, surging ceaselessly over feet and knees and bags and stray children. Penny felt her face begin to burn in embarrassment even though the hubbub wasn't her fault. The only good thing was that those who had been sitting behind Agatha could now see the stage, their view unimpeded by the towering beehive.

"How are you, my love?" Agatha boomed as she sailed nearer.

"Very well, thank you. Er. Now then, and all that."

Agatha snorted with laughter at Penny's attempt to casually use some Lincolnshire dialect. "Keep working at it," she said. "We'll rough up the edges of your London ways sooner or later." She settled down next to Penny.

"It goes both ways. Perhaps I'll smooth all of you locals out a little," Penny retorted.

A man who was sitting in front of them half-turned around. "Won't happen," he declared, his vowels long and rounded. "You'll become one of us." He smiled. "Well, in about five generations, that is." He turned away and began to talk to his neighbour about the weather, although all they could really say was "it's rather hot, but then, it is July."

"Who was that?" Penny hissed, leaning in to Agatha's ample shoulder.

"I have no idea," Agatha said back, with no volume control at all. "Just some man being friendly, eh?"

By telling me I won't be local until the kids – which I don't and won't have – are great-grandparents, she thought. *Huh.* Penny folded her arms mock-grumpily and sighed.

"Is that dog of yours still giving you gyp, eh?" Agatha asked kindly, misinterpreting Penny's body language.

Penny shook her head. "No, she's doing all right now," she said, somewhat defensively. Even though she'd owned Kali for a good few months, and the rescue dog's more extreme reactions to random things, other dogs, men in hats, and people carrying bags was now calming down, she still felt protective of her. "No. It's just that my friend from London has come to stay and she doesn't seem to be making any plans to leave."

The strange man, unashamedly eavesdropping, turned around again. "Just like fish," he informed them.

"What, fish don't make plans to leave?" Penny said.

"Well, they don't," Agatha said thoughtfully. "They just go. You know, when they swim upstream. Is it all fish, do you think? Or is it just salmon that do that?"

"No," the man said. "I mean, it's that proverb. House guests are like fish. After three days, they begin to stink."

"You do let her use the bathroom, don't you?" Agatha said. "It's awfully hot ..."

Penny rolled her eyes. "Of course I do. And Francine is lovely, and that's probably the problem, because she's all sweetness and light and I feel like I can't have a good rant while she's there, because she gets upset on behalf of ... of everything in the world. I can't even watch the news anymore. It makes her weepy. I've never signed so many petitions as I have done in the last week."

The man rolled his eyes in return, and turned away once more. Penny knew that he was thinking she ought to just tell Francine to go.

But Francine had turned up, out of the blue, with two large suitcases and a determination to "change her destiny." She'd packed in her job and declared that Penny was her "inspiration" and that she'd use her example to "manifest a new life."

Penny felt oddly responsible. What would happen if this new life and sparkling destiny didn't manifest itself?

She had a sneaking suspicion that she would have let Francine down. Somehow. In an irrational way.

But then, much about Francine was irrational. It was what made her so appealing. She had a joyous exuberant approach to life that Penny had always secretly envied. To some extent, Francine's buoyant nature had inspired Penny to start *her* new life.

Francine's willingness to be open to the "leadings and promptings of the Great Universe" meant she often found meaning in small things. She once drove the long way home just because she'd seen a leaf swirling to the ground, taking many seconds to make its journey. Her insights were simple and naïve, and sometimes bonkers.

Though at least she didn't go in for crystals and fairies, like Lucy at the dogs' home.

Penny winced. Those pair must never meet, she decided. There'd be some kind of cosmic event and metaphysical glitter would rain down upon the small town of Upper Glenfield.

"I don't watch the news either," Agatha said, bringing Penny sharply out of her reverie.

"Sorry," she said. "I was miles away." Who was

watching the news?

Oh yes, not her, because of Francine.

Agatha patted her knee like an elderly aunt. "There, there."

Penny smiled and appreciated the older woman's misplaced sympathy. She craned her neck and glanced around, keen for the meeting to begin. "I can see a few folks from the arts group," she said. "There's Mary. Where's Ginni, though? And the councillors? Wasn't the meeting supposed to have started by now? I'm really looking forward to seeing all the plans."

Agatha's eyebrows shot up. "Haven't you heard? Ginni won't be coming! Not now, eh. Not what with all what's happened."

"Why ever not?" Ginni was in charge of the local arts and crafts group. Penny often went to the group's meetings, although now that she was selling much of her textile art and small watercolour paintings, she felt a little awkward. Some folks seemed to think she was a "proper" artist and asked her for feedback on their own work, which was a delicate and fraught activity. When many people asked for honest criticism, what they actually wanted was praise. She learned that quickly, and painfully, and it had taken a lot of cake to smooth out the ruffled egos.

Agatha pressed her hands together, rings clinking, and spoke with relish. "Well, it's a done deal, isn't it? The town council have already decided who the sculptor is going to be, and that's why Ginni's so upset. It was all hush hush and closed doors stuff. I smell some dodgy goings-on ... maybe even money changed hands! Oh – now, here they come at last."

The murmuring in the hall rose and then faded, like a tidal wave that ebbed away, as two men and one woman clattered their way to the front of the hall. Penny recognised Shaun Kapowski, the local butcher, but she didn't know the other two.

"Thank you all for coming," Shaun said, as the two others sat down and smiled awkwardly over the tops of everyone's heads, staring at the back of the hall. Shaun had a loud voice at complete odds with his small and slight figure. No one who had seen him wrestle half a pig out of the back of a lorry would doubt the power contained in his tiny frame, however. His energy matched his voice not his body. He was like a tightly compressed goblin. "We apologise for the delay. We are just waiting for our artist to arrive."

"We haven't decided who the artist is yet, have we?" shouted one voice from the middle of the hall. "We all want to see the designs."

"Of course, of course," Shaun said. "And we are delighted by the interest that the residents of Upper Glenfield have shown in this project. We could not do this without your support. However, the committee has had to face some complex funding issues and..."

Penny knew as soon as Shaun had switched from saying "we" to "the committee" that they were in for an onslaught of political double-speak, and soon everyone's eyes were glazing over as he explained why the decision had already been made, and the conditions of the central government grant they'd been awarded, and the unexpected deadline for the funding, and how exciting and vibrant and forward-thinking and wonderful the town council was.

Eventually Shaun petered out, and looked to his companions. They, too, were frowning, and glancing about the hall and then at their watches.

The assembled crowd picked up on the uncertainty,

and began to whisper to one another.

Agatha, lacking her volume control again, said, "Looks like someone's gone and goofed up, doesn't it, eh? I wonder who we're waiting for."

The man in front of them turned again. "I heard it was that weirdo, Alec what's-his-face, him that never talks to anyone. Him as lives down South Road. Probably eats squirrels. He looks the type."

"Alec Goodwin?" Agatha sucked at her teeth. "It might be. But he never gets involved in anything like this. Poor Ginni. She had such hopes for her nephew."

The man shook his head. "What? I don't rate him, neither. That kid is a wrong 'un and I wouldn't trust him as far as I could throw him, except I wouldn't throw him because I wouldn't want to touch him to pick him up. Maybe with gloves on. I'd throw him if I was wearing gloves."

"Who is Alec Goodwin?" Penny asked, trying to steer the conversation back into saner waters. She thought she had heard the name before, but it was getting mixed up with Ginni's nephew now, and she was already lost.

And she didn't get an answer because at that moment,

the double doors at the back of the hall burst open, and a young man with lank straw-like hair burst in and shouted,

"Alec Goodwin's dead!"

CHAPTER TWO

The hall exploded. Penny didn't move. She sat still, quite stunned waiting to see what would happen next. Agatha got to her feet though it didn't make the diminutive woman a great deal taller. The chatty man in front of them stood up too, and he moved towards the crowd that was gathering around the young man who'd delivered the shocking news.

Agatha tried to push forward, but soon realised she'd get nowhere. She turned around to face Penny who was still seated. "What a to-do. You'll be thinking that he was murdered, I suppose! Eh?" she said.

"Of course not. Not *everyone* who dies around here is murdered." *I'm not some kind of curse that's happening to Upper Glenfield,* she thought, slightly resentfully. *Even if the local homicide rate has tripled since I've lived here. That's sheer co-incidence and can't be blamed on my presence.* "Who is he, anyway? I have heard the name."

"Alec Goodwin? Like that bloke said, he's a strange sort of man. But he's a celebrated artist, you know. He almost certainly does *not* eat squirrels."

Penny made the connection. She vaguely recollected hearing of a reclusive sculptor that lived in the town. "Is he … was he … old?"

"Not really. Sixty or so? Not, you know, *elderly* kind of old."

Sixty wasn't old, Penny realised with a sad shock. Not now that she herself was the other side of forty. Sixty wasn't too far down the list of fast-approaching significant birthdays. "And who's that lad?" she asked. "The one who came in with the news. I think I have seen him recently, hanging around the market with those other kids, smoking and being loud." *Like I was once,* she reminded herself. *Don't be mean. Kids are just kids.*

"Oh, him." Agatha glanced around, and attempted to lower her voice. "That would be Steve Llewellyn. Ginni's nephew, you know. She was so keen for him to present his ideas for the Sculpture Trail."

Penny frowned. "Really? How old is he?"

"He's just finished at University. What would that make him? Twenty-one or so, eh?"

"Wow. He looks about nineteen." *And behaves about that age, too.*

Agatha sniffed. "And he's as scruffy as they come. He needs to smarten up if he expects to get a job out there in the real world. You have to learn to toe the corporate line and not stand out, eh." She ran her blood-red fingernails over her unconventional beehive, and twisted her neck to see what was happening.

Penny got to her feet decisively. "I'm going to take a closer look at him. People seem awfully excited about all this."

"Of course they are!" Agatha said. "Obviously, a man dead, sad loss and all that. But after all this, who will take over the Sculpture Trail now?"

The obvious candidate, Penny thought, was Steve, who had been passed over. She pressed her lips together and began to elbow her way through the chattering crowd.

* * * *

Closer up, she saw that the young man was, indeed, in his early twenties. He still had a youthful lankiness to his limbs but his shoulders were beginning to broaden out. His hair was unkempt and came to his jawline in ragged clumps which screamed of split ends, and he hadn't shaved for a few days. Whether that was a fashion statement, or simple slovenliness, Penny didn't like to guess.

He looked like he might smell a bit musty, and she chided herself for her judgemental thought, but once it was in her head, it wasn't leaving. If people did have auras, she'd assume his would be beige-tinged.

Now she was close enough to hear what he was saying.

"I dunno! I dunno, all right!" He was shaking his head angrily. "I just come here to tell you all what I saw, that's all."

"Shouldn't you have waited for the police and the ambulance to arrive?" a woman said.

Steve's eyes were wide and glistening. "I weren't gonna wait there, next to a body all dead and that! Oh, no. He were dead! He were all stiff!" He added in a few expletives.

He might have just graduated, Penny thought, *but it wasn't with a degree in English.* She wondered where he had studied, as he hadn't lost a single scrap of his broad local accent.

"Did you touch him?" someone asked.

"Of course I didn't touch him!" The poor lad was genuinely distressed. "He were … urgh. Like, laid out on the ground. He were a funny colour, blue and white and red, and there was all this sick everywhere…"

Everyone gasped and recoiled, and rather ghoulishly, everyone wanted to know even more details. "Did you see anything else suspicious?" Shaun, the council leader, asked.

"Suspicious? What, like, *apart* from a corpse?" Steve shot back.

"Was there anyone around? Did you see any vehicles? Anything?"

Someone else butted in, saying, "Surely the police will ask him that sort of thing. We're probably interfering with enquiries or something."

"Yeah," Steve said. His fists were tight little balls of stretched white skin. "But anyway, I didn't see nothing. Nothing! Just some old dirty van, and a shabby hatchback. And that were it."

"What colour was the van?"

Steve was not coping with the pressure of being

harangued and questioned from all sides. "I *dunno!*" he bawled. "Red. Reddish-brown. No, white. Whatever. I just came to tell you all. I just came to tell my aunt. I want to talk to my aunt. Where is she?"

"She's not here," various people said, all masters and mistresses of the obvious.

Steve stared about wildly, and without a further word, began to push through the crowd to the doors at the back of the hall. People called after him, barracking him with loud and insistent questions, but he ignored them all, and slammed the doors hard back as he shot through them and away into the gathering dusk.

"Well now," said Agatha, appearing at Penny's side like an apparition. "Why would he think that his aunt was here, eh?"

"Well, *I* thought she was going to be here," Penny pointed out. "She's pretty prominent in the local arts scene."

"True, but Steve is living with Ginni at the moment. He moved in once his final term ended the other week. That's why she's so keen to get him gainfully employed, you might say."

"But Ginni lives in that tiny flat above her floristry shop!"

"Exactly. There's hardly room for one up there, never mind two." Agatha sucked her teeth. "Now I do wonder, of course, what that Steve was doing down at Alec Goodwin's house in the first place."

"Where is Alec's house?" Penny asked. "South Road, that man said…"

"Right the way down South Road," Agatha told her. "You go past the pub on the roundabout and you keep on going, until you run out of houses. And you go on a bit further, and it's there, behind a load of tall conifers."

That was so typical of Lincolnshire, Penny thought. There were huge, detached houses scattered all over the farming area, hidden away behind trees and hedges.

"Is it on the way to anywhere? Could Steve have been passing by, quite innocently?"

Agatha blurted out a laugh, and a few eavesdroppers that were nearby also laughed. "No, my love, no. It's the real back of beyond. It's not the sort of place you'd go even if you wanted to."

"But that makes no …" Penny stopped and shook her head. Agatha didn't always make sense. She understood what the hairdresser meant.

The man who had been turning around and talking to them before was still close by. He said, "Happen he was down there seeing that Barry chap."

Penny ran the Lincolnshire dialect through her mental dictionary. *Steve might have been visiting someone called Barry.* "Who's Barry?"

"Oh, he's just a farm labourer that rents a cottage next to Alec's house," Agatha told her. "I say a 'cottage.' Actually it's a prefab place, should have been knocked down after the war. You wouldn't keep chickens in it, but there we go. Barry's part of the scenery around here. He wouldn't hurt a fly, would Barry. He's one of nature's children, if you know what I mean, eh?"

"No, not really." Penny mentally added Barry to her shortlist and then reminded herself that no one even knew if Alec's death had been foul play.

People were forming into small groups, and all the chatter that she could overhear was about Steve and Alec. Why had Steve been there? How had Alec died?

And why had Steve run to the meeting with the news, instead of staying with the body for the authorities to arrive?

The speculation became circular, as things did when

there was no new information. Penny bid Agatha farewell, and began to walk slowly back to her cottage.

Very slowly.

Francine would be there, being all cheerful and sweetness and keen.

But then, Penny reminded herself, her dog Kali would also be waiting for her. She picked up the pace again.

* * * *

Penny's cottage was one of a row, all built in warm yellow stone that had been quarried locally some fifty years previously. The road, River Street, was a dead end, and tended to be quiet although there was a footpath at the far end that led down to the river, where young people would gather on warm evenings, laughing and sneakily drinking and pretending to be rebels. The cottages didn't have front yards. They faced directly onto the pavement, but out at the back of the cottages, they had long gardens that ran to an alleyway. Penny's small car was parked out at the front of her cottage, and her frivolously-purchased classic motorbike and sidecar was in the shed at the bottom of her back garden.

And next to her own car was Francine's little red hatchback. Penny stopped on the pavement and gazed at her front door.

But her moment of reflection was immediately interrupted by a barrage of barking. Penny winced and made a silent apology to her neighbours. How did Kali know that Penny was standing outside? Francine would tell her that they were in tune with one another because they'd "bonded" but she had also starting referring to Penny as "Kali's mummy" which Penny found both odd and awkward.

The front door opened and Francine's beaming face appeared above the delightful apparition of foaming, barking dog. Kali shot out, tail blurring, and butted into Penny, almost twisting herself into a spiral in her eagerness to greet her owner. She wanted to simultaneously press against Penny, lie down for a belly rub, and run in a circle. She tried to do all three, and nearly fell over. Penny knew that her daft Rottweiler would never be entering any agility competitions. She'd fallen backwards off the sofa more than once.

"I told you she was coming back," Francine said to the over-excited dog.

Penny patted Kali once, and stood up straight. "It's not good for her to get so wound up," she said. "I can usually come and go without her making a big fuss."

Francine didn't look at Penny. She was holding her arms out to Kali and making "shush" noises. Kali, quite understandably, didn't like the outstretched hand which looked like a bit of a threat to her, and the noise Francine was making was unsettling. So Kali stayed by Penny, leaning back against her legs, and making a snuffling noise of greeting.

Francine looked hurt. She sighed and stood up to face Penny, brushing her hands together. "Well. So how was the sculpture meeting? Did you get to see lots of exciting designs? What are they going to do? When will it be completed? Is it fantastic?"

Penny stroked the top of Kali's head. She didn't want to talk. She wanted to sift it all in her mind and mull it over for a while. She'd always lived alone, more or less, and was set in her ways.

But Francine was smiling in an open and disarming way. Penny didn't want to seem rude or churlish.

"An artist *had* been chosen," Penny said. "And some

people were quite upset, because the council did it secretly and in advance. It's all irrelevant now, though. He seems to have suffered some … uh, misfortune."

"Oh? How so?"

"He's dead, apparently."

Francine's hand flew to her mouth in a dramatic yet – for her – totally natural movement. Her usually narrow eyes widened. "No! How and when? Right there, at the meeting? Oh gosh. How awful for him, and you all. Was it a heart attack?"

"Not quite. He didn't actually make it to the meeting. It was a man called Alec Goodwin."

Francine's mouth closed and opened. "Alec Horatio Goodwin," she said.

"How do you know that?"

"He's a famous sculptor. He lives here in Upper Glenfield. Surely you know that!"

Now Penny was as curious as Francine had been. "Since when were you into sculpture?" Penny and Francine had worked together on television productions in London, but Francine had never seemed the cultural type.

"Since I moved here, and did some research about the

personalities of the local area," Francine said.

"*Moved* here?"

Even sweet Francine could pick up on Penny's tone. Her smile wavered. "Well, you know what I mean. Anyway. I am sure Kali would love a walk! Walkies! Walkies, Kali, walkies!" Her voice rose higher and higher, and Kali remained pressed to Penny's leg, her brow furrowed and ears pricked forward.

"She would love a walk," Penny said. "I'll just go grab her lead."

"Oh, let me." Francine darted back into the hallway and picked the lead off the hook behind the door. She passed it to Penny and said, "And I'll just go fetch my shoes, and –"

Penny clipped the lead to Kali's collar and began to retreat as if she hadn't heard Francine. She had. And she felt like a terrible person. But she desperately needed some space.

"I won't be long," she trilled with a falsely cheerful voice. "I may as well make the most of this lovely evening. See you soon!"

* * * *

She *had* to walk along South Road, in the direction of Alec Goodwin's house. She was driven to it. She didn't even pretend to herself that it was anything other than pure, naked curiosity on her part.

The light was fading but she wasn't worried, even when the sparse street lights petered out. It would not be full dark for some time yet, and the three-quarter moon was already rising. Kali stopped to sniff the new and exciting clumps of grass that she hadn't ever sniffed before, and her tail wagged in delight from time to time when she discovered something particularly rank and smelly. Penny didn't like to look too closely.

She was going to have a proper sit-down chat with Francine, she decided. She didn't want to hurt her feelings, but it was time for her to leave.

She wasn't entirely clear on why Francine had come. "Manifesting one's destiny" sounded like something you'd say to yourself rather than a painful truth. There had to be more to it, and it was one reason why Penny was treading carefully. On the one hand, she needed to let Francine reveal her real reasons in her own time.

But on the other hand, Penny wanted her cottage back.

Penny tried out various scenarios in her head, but they all seemed to end with Francine in floods of tears.

Her mind was so pre-occupied with the right course of action that she didn't notice Kali was stressed out about something until the dog lunged forward, dragging the lead from her hands. With a wild yelp, she plunged into a hedge, her tail thrashing from side to side.

"Kali! No!" she yelled, and then remembered the positive training she was supposed to be doing. *Tell the dog what you do want, not what you don't.* "Kali - sit!"

The dog's tail thrashed once more and her hindquarters disappeared into the foliage.

CHAPTER THREE

"Kali! Come here!" Penny stopped and took a step back. She had to keep her voice calm and upbeat, she reminded herself. Kali was a much better behaved and more relaxed dog these days, but she had a long way to go yet before she'd win any prizes at a behaviour class. Penny should have noticed the warning signs; it was her own fault, and directing anger at the dog was pointless. Dogs did dog things. Penny was still learning about dog training. She knew she had to sound happy. After all, as the knowledgeable man in the rambling group had told her, who would run towards someone who sounded angry?

It made sense. Penny could see that there was only a field of crops on the other side of the hedge, so she wasn't worried about Kali wreaking havoc upon livestock. "Kali! I have lots of yummy treats," she announced in a sing song voice. "Come here, Kaliiiiiiii. Come on, girl. Let's go!"

There was a rustling, a growl, some scuffles and then a black nose pushed through the hedge, followed by the rest of the dog. She looked sheepishly to the floor, expecting to be berated and shouted at. She was a rescue dog, with an unpleasant past, and her submission to humans always broke Penny's heart.

"Oh, come here," Penny said, dropping to her knees. She fished around in her pocket for a soft treat. Her hands smelled of tripe most of the time, these days. There was also a smudge on the thighs of most of her walking trousers, where she'd constantly wipe her hands clear of dog drool.

Kali looked at Penny sideways and licked her lips in nervousness, but when she caught the scent of the meaty snack, she perked up and licked her lips in genuine anticipation. As soon as she was close enough, Penny gave her the treat and lots of reassuring petting. There was no point in telling her off now; she wouldn't connect the punishment with what had gone on just a few moments previously.

"What was all that about?" Penny mused. Then she spotted the ragged remnants of a white carrier bag in the hedge. It made sense. Kali hated them and would still flinch when anyone walked past her carrying a similar bag.

"Come on, you. Happy now?"

Kali looked up, mouth open and tongue lolling.

Dogs lived in the moment, and it was a fine pattern to follow.

* * * *

It was easy to find the right house. After all, there was a rather obvious police cordon outside. There was a police car parked up on the grassy verge, a police van on the verge opposite, and blue and white tape stretched across the gateway that was flanked by high hedges.

She recognised PC Patel who was standing by the tape. He blanched slightly when he saw her, but he quickly plastered a professional smile on to greet her.

"Good evening, Ms May."

"Hi, there. Um. Look. About that biscuit I gave you, all those months ago. I'm sorry. I never got the chance to apologise for ever-so-slightly poisoning you..."

"No, no, no. It's fine. It's all forgotten."

She grinned. "If I had known you were here, I would have brought you a cake to say sorry properly…"

A female voice spoke sternly from behind PC Patel. "Stop teasing my constable."

"Cath! Sorry. I should call you DC Pritchard. You're all official."

"I am." Cath Pritchard grinned back. She was in plain clothes, just a smart dark trouser suit that was well fitted to her matronly figure. "I wondered how long it would take for you to turn up."

"Well, as I was of such assistance last time, I thought my presence would be welcomed."

"Not with the dog, I'm afraid. Hello, Kali."

"I'm just here to look," Penny said.

"Of course, and I think that you can, at least from a distance. I think the Inspector's special dispensation from last time was never revoked, was it? Not officially revoked, as it was never officially given. It's just that we have our own dogs working part of the area, though." Cath nodded at Kali. "She can stay with PC Patel. You like dogs, don't you?"

"I *tolerate* dogs," he said stiffly. "I prefer cats."

"She's friendly," Penny said, holding out the lead to the young policeman. "I know she's a Rottweiler but she does love people. Generally. Just don't wave a white carrier bag at her, that's all."

PC Patel looked startled but took the lead, and Penny ducked under the blue and white tape, following Cath along a neglected and weed-strewn gravel driveway.

Penny was bursting with questions, but she managed to bite her tongue. She looked around for a moment, absorbing what she saw, wanting to get a feel for the place where Alec had lived. Ahead of them was a square, boxy house in red brick, with a door in the dead centre and two windows either side. Upstairs were two more windows. The wooden frames had blue paint, peeling and cracked. It looked just like a child's drawing of what a house should be. All it needed was a smiling yellow sun hanging above it.

"I'm surprised," Penny said. "It looks really small."

"It is," Cath said. "Everyone thought he was a rich genius, but really, he was neither rich nor ... well, I don't rate his art. I suppose you heard about all this while you were at the Sculpture Trail meeting? We've had lots of busy-bodies come nosing down here in the past hour."

"Yeah. A young man called Steve burst in. He's Ginni the florist's nephew. Everyone's talking about why he was here in the first place, and why he ran away."

"It is a bit strange, why he was here. But as for running off – that's normal. People panic and act in all sorts of ways."

Penny paused. "He also mentioned there was a van here as well as a car. Where is it?" She could only see a car, a small hatchback.

"There wasn't any van here. That's Alec's little car, there. Did he give a description of the van?"

"Not really. He said it was red, then changed his mind and said it was white."

"That," said Cath, "sounds very suspicious. But he was in a panic when he made the call. It has freaked him out a lot, from what I hear. He can have some counselling, if he likes, at some point."

They walked around the side of the house, and Penny saw there was a single-storey building at the far end of the long, overgrown garden. The building was made from prefab concrete sheets, and had a tin roof. It looked like the emergency housing the government had encouraged to be built after the second world war, but those structures were never intended to be used for more than ten years. The grey walls had dark patches blooming across them, and it didn't look very safe or appealing. It was bordered by a plain chain-link fence, six feet high, and it had the whiff of a prison about it. Somewhere, a dog was barking. Penny turned back to look at the main house. They were now standing on a green and cracked patio.

"This is his studio," said Cath, and she waved at a long room like a conservatory that was tacked onto the back of his house. Like the windows and doors, the main framework was built in wood, and it seemed to be single-glazed. "What do you know about the deceased?"

"Not a lot," Penny confessed. "And what I do know, I only learned today at the meeting. He was called Alec Goodwin, he was a sculptor, Francine thinks he was famous, and he kept himself to himself. He probably didn't eat squirrels. Oh, and he was found dead by Steve."

"He was found over there," Cath said, and pointed to a screened-off area. It was on the edge of the lawn, where the patio ended.

Penny's flesh tingled. "Oh. Is he still ... behind there?"

"No, he's gone off for all the usual tests and so on. But the forensics bods are behind that screen, doing their wizardry, so you can't go there. We're not sure if the death is suspicious, yet, to be honest, but we can't take any chances until we know for sure."

"What's in that place behind the fence? That shed," Penny asked.

"A man called Barry Neville lives there. He rents it from Alec Goodwin."

"Wow. Someone *lives* there? Is that even legal? It looks like it's going to fall down. This Alec guy wasn't much of a landlord, was he?"

Cath shook her head. "He wasn't much of a homeowner, full stop. Come into the studio. Touch *nothing*."

They stepped off the patio, and into the long conservatory. The lights were on, and moths were buzzing around. It smelled of turpentine and oils and wood and glue, and stirred Penny's happy memories of her art student days. She inhaled deeply. "Aah."

Cath looked at her in horror. "Urgh, more like."

Penny ignored her. She walked slowly through the

chaos and debris of a working artist's studio, itching to open the cupboards and flick through the sketchbooks. "He wasn't just a sculptor, was he?" she said. There were canvases, stretched over wooden frames, stacked up against a wall, some as tall as she was. Palettes with caked-on paint littered a long bench along one wall. Everywhere there were stained mugs and cups with brushes sticking out of them. There was also a table with clay figures laid out to dry on boards. They seemed to be animal shapes, but stylised and simple, reminding her of the bold forms of Brancusi and even Henry Moore. She liked them more than his paintings, which were dark, and had great slashes of red and black across them.

"No," Cath said. "You're right. He did all kinds of art." She came to stand next to Penny as they both contemplated his current work. It was a large square canvas mounted on an easel.

"And did he make his living selling this stuff?" Penny asked.

"I think so. We don't know much about him. Hopefully you and your gossip-radar can pick up on some information around the town. I do know he used to be a courtroom artist, but he came here years ago and has lived in seclusion ever since, all alone, but for Barry out there in that shack with his dogs."

"Do they even have courtroom artists anymore? Don't they just take photos?"

Cath laughed. "You can't take a camera into a UK court. And, actually, you can't draw while the court is in session, either. All the courtroom sketches you see in newspapers were done afterwards, by the artist, from their memory."

"That is impressive."

"Yeah. You'd think he'd be better at drawing, wouldn't you?"

"What do you mean?"

Cath pointed at the work in front of them. "It's a bit … I don't know. Scrappy. I wouldn't have it on *my* wall. Perhaps the guest bedroom. For when people I didn't like came to visit."

Penny sighed. "You don't appreciate art."

"I guess I don't have a degree in it. Why can't things just look nice? I like flowers."

The work in progress was a mixed-media piece, with

collage and paint and pastels, all jumbled up together, and the dark searing lines of angry charcoal showing through the paint in places. There were some headlines torn from newspapers, and a recurring theme of a woman's face. She had a long nose and dark bobbed hair, and stared through slitted eyes directly at the viewer.

"But you're right," Penny conceded. "I don't like it, either, and I don't think it's very good. It's a bit overcooked. Like a first-year art student trying too hard to be intense and emotional and dangerous."

"Oh, so you're allowed to say it's rubbish because you're trained?"

Penny grinned. "Yeah, that's about it."

Cath moved away to stare at the clay models on the table, but Penny stayed transfixed by the art. It made her shiver. She definitely didn't like it. Perhaps, she argued with herself, this meant it was successful because it had created an emotion in her. That's what artists wanted, after all – a reaction.

Something about the emerging image bugged her. She felt as if she had seen it before. She tried to read the newspaper headlines on the torn scraps that were glued to the canvas, but they were a mundane mix of local news and celebrity gossip, with no apparent hidden meaning, as far as she could tell.

The woman, her image repeated a few times across the canvas in varying sizes, still glared out at Penny. Penny rubbed her upper arms with her hands, and stepped across to join Cath. "It's getting cold," she said, as if that would explain her sudden goose-bumps.

"I don't think this place even has central heating," Cath said. "We're still going through the rest of the house so I can't let you in there. Shall we go back outside?"

"Please."

They stepped out onto the patio, but the night air was now clouded with midges and irritating biting insects. Penny swiped at her face. "You will want to know the general chatter around town, won't you?"

"Yes please, just in case this turns out to be unusual. You're *not* investigating, okay? But I think the fact that he was about to take on the Sculpture Trail makes me suspicious."

"He was a recluse, anyway. Why would he agree to it?" Penny said. "Had he done anything like that before?"

"Not that we know of, but see if you can find out. I suppose he needed the money, but we're going to get access to his private affairs over the next few days."

Penny looked down at where the weeds were pushing up through the cracks in the patio. "It looks to me like he certainly needed the cash."

"Oh, he'll probably turn out to be one of those who lives in poverty but who has a stack of millions under the bed. Honestly, it really happens."

"Let me know if that's the case," Penny said, as she turned to go. "You can discretely shuffle half a million or so in my direction. No one would miss it, would they?"

"If that happens," Cath said, "you can be assured that suddenly this apparently friendless and family-free man would be crawling with long-lost relatives. Hey, are you free tomorrow night?"

"Sure. Do you want to meet up? You can come around if you like."

"I will. I should have news for you by then."

"Me too."

Penny raised her hand in farewell and went to rescue PC Patel from Kali. He surrendered the dog to her with a grateful smile.

"Did you make friends?" she asked the policeman.

"She's covered my trousers in drool," he said morosely.

"Does it wash off?"

"Eventually."

CHAPTER FOUR

By the time that Penny got home that night, Francine had already taken herself off to bed in the spare room. Penny made a quiet cup of herbal tea and sat up for a while, curled on her sofa with Kali snoring at the other end in her nest of cushions. She pondered the events of the day but came to no fixed conclusions, before deciding to turn in for the night.

She slept fitfully.

The next morning, Penny was up and out of the house, walking Kali in the fresh early air while it was still cool. Hot weather and thick black fur didn't mix. She was also avoiding Francine. Now she'd made her mind up to definitely have a heart to heart chat with her, she felt deeply reluctant to take the next step and make her intentions into reality.

She had a chance when she returned from the walk. Francine was sitting in the kitchen, a few glossy magazines spread open on the table. She smiled and jumped to her feet.

"Penny! You're back! I'll get the kettle on," she said.

"Ahh … maybe later," Penny blurted out. She didn't even know she was going to refuse the offer until she heard herself speaking. "I'm popping out to the market."

"Oh, I'll –"

Penny grabbed her purse and left.

It must be obvious to Francine, now, she thought, and had a pang of guilt, pausing in the hallway. *I could ask her to come with me.*

Then she heard Francine begin to talk to Kali. "Let's do some tricks!"

No, I won't disturb her, Penny thought, and continued out the door.

* * * *

Anyway, Penny said to herself as she tried to justify her own unappealing behaviour, *I need to start finding out about*

Alec Goodwin. What better place to start than the market?

The town of Upper Glenfield was a thriving one, and had a permanent indoor market as well as a weekly outdoor event. She reached the end of her street and crossed the road, and from there it was just a short walk along the High Street to the market area. The indoor market had a wide variety of stalls selling local produce as well as all the usual strange market goods like nylon aprons and plastic buckets and gadgets for unblocking sinks that would break after the first attempt. She waved and nodded at the familiar faces she saw. Often, she knew the stallholders well enough to chat to, but she had not ever established what their names were. Now she'd lived here for a few months, it felt too awkwardly late to ask what they were called. In her head, she started referring to them by what they sold. There was Mop Woman, Fish Man, and of course, Book Man With The Pimples.

She headed for Book Man With The Pimples, but was waylaid almost immediately by Mary who was coming away from the book stall clutching a lurid romance with a fainting woman on the pink and purple cover. "Penny! Now then."

"Hi, Mary. How are the craft fairs going?"

"We miss you," Mary said. She was dressed in many layers of purple and each layer had an edging of lace. She was like a doily that had exploded. "Well, I miss you, anyway."

It sounded like the others didn't miss her, and that was probably correct. Penny had attended quite a few local craft fairs with her textile art and watercolour paintings, but she'd been unprepared for the resentment that a scant handful of established crafters had harboured for newcomers. Now she was selling more of her work from her website, she had scaled back how many craft fairs she attended, but Mary was still keen. She hardly sold any of her terrible decoupage, but she kept going for the social scene. Mary had never been perceived as a threat by the others, though.

Mary was bursting with gossip, as always. Before Penny could say anything else about the craft fairs, she went on. "And have you heard about Alec Goodwin? What a business, what a business! Dreadful shock."

"I heard that he was found dead, yes," Penny said, hoping that Mary would fill in some of the gaps.

"Murdered, no doubt about it!"

"Do you know that for sure?"

"Well ... no, but that's what they're all saying."

Penny raised one eyebrow and Mary did look slightly embarrassed. Gossip had got her into a lot of trouble when Penny had moved to Upper Glenfield, and it had cost the older woman many friends, too. "Mary, do you know anything about Alec Goodwin? Why had he been picked to do the Sculpture Trail?"

"Oh, he was always being asked to do this and that. He was almost a local celebrity. He never said yes to anything before, though."

"So, why this one?"

"He probably needed the money. Starving artists never have any money. They spend it all on absinthe. I know they all say he was rich and that, but me, I don't think so."

Alec's poverty sounded plausible to Penny after having seen the state of disrepair that his house was in. "I wonder what will happen to the Sculpture Trail now," she said, leaving it open and hoping Mary would fill in more gaps.

She did. "This morning, that council man, Shaun, went to see Ginni in the florists', and asked her to take it on!" Mary announced, beaming at the delight of imparting new knowledge. "And apparently ... she said no."

"I'm not surprised she said no. I know Ginni runs the craft group, but I've never seen her do any art or craft except her floral creations," Penny said. "Which are stunning, by the way, but I can't imagine her doing sculptures. Is that her background?"

"I don't know. That's not why she refused, though," Mary said. "She said no out of spite and resentment because the council didn't choose her nephew, either in the first place, or now, as a replacement. She's very bitter about it."

"Hmm." Ginni was an old-school dragon of a woman who could still rock a pair of shoulder-pads like it was 1988, but Penny hadn't pegged her for someone who held a grudge. Then again, where family was concerned, people were unpredictable. She asked, "Did Alec have any family?"

"I have no idea," Mary said. "I never heard of any. But if I find out, I'll let you know. I imagine you're going to snoop around for clues now, aren't you?"

"We don't know for sure how he died, yet."

"Well, no. But as I said …"

Penny smiled. "I know, I know. Everyone thinks it's murder. Thanks, Mary."

She bid her farewell and continued to wander around

the market.

* * * *

Penny picked up some vegetables from Knobbly Potatoes Man and decided she'd make a nice spicy vegetarian stew that evening. She was on her way back to her cottage when Cath called her, so she stopped and rested in the shade of the churchyard wall while she chatted on her mobile phone.

"Hey there," Cath said. "I'm on a break and I thought I'd let you know that we've been talking to Steve Llewellyn, Ginni's nephew. Have you met him properly at all?"

"I saw him last night when he burst into the meeting, and I've seen him hanging around, but that's it."

"Right. So we were interested to find out why he had been down at Alec's place," Cath said.

"Everyone wants to know that."

"Apparently, he'd been there drinking with Barry Neville the previous night."

"Barry? The guy that rents the shack on Alec's property? Are they friends?"

"It seems ... unlikely, but Steve reckons they are. Inspector Travis is inclined to believe it, too. Barry's in his thirties. He's a farm labourer, on casual contracts here and there. Sometimes, factory work, when the farm work is low. And Steve is just out of university. So I dunno, there's more to it that Steve's not saying. Anyway, Steve said that he had been there with Barry on Saturday night, getting drunk and trying to teach Barry's dogs some tricks, and he left his phone there. So on Sunday he went back down to get it back."

"He didn't go back for his phone until Sunday night?" Penny shook her head even though Cath couldn't see her. "I don't buy that. Kids these days are welded to their phones."

"Maybe, maybe not. I don't think we can lump all 'kids' together. There's another thing, as well," Cath told her. "Steve said that he walked there. Fair enough. It's not too far. But – I remember you said that Steve said there had been a van there that night? Well, we have another witness, someone who was out for a jog along that road, who noticed a van pull out of the gateway. He noticed it because of the erratic driving. He had had to jump up onto the verge."

54

"Was the van red or white?"

"Both. White, but filthy with dust, the jogger said. And it was around the time the body was discovered, give or take."

Penny pondered for a moment. "You say Steve had been drinking," she said. "That would explain the erratic driving."

"It would also explain why he said he had walked there," Cath added. "So that he didn't get looked at for drink-driving, although it would be too late to charge him with that. There'd be no proof."

"Does Steve have a van?" Penny asked.

"He has access to his aunt's. She has a white van for her floristry business."

"Oh." Penny let her breath out in a long exhale. Things weren't looking too good for the young arts graduate. "Has there been any progress on Alec's cause of death?"

"Not yet," Cath said. "But I hope to have more news when I come round tonight. I expect a bottle of wine to be chilling in the fridge."

"It's proportional to how much information you bring me," Penny informed her. "You might have to make do with a flat lemonade…"

* * * *

The rest of Monday was a strange, unsettled sort of day. Penny had resolved to talk with Francine about her plans, but when she got home, Francine was out. She'd left a short note about "following her heart" which Penny took to mean that she was browsing around the pleasant shops of the cathedral city of Lincoln, which lay to the north of Upper Glenfield. Penny felt relief and also let down, as she had steeled herself for the expected confrontation.

Instead, she applied herself to her website. There were some enquiries to respond to, and some new images to upload. This was only *semi*-retirement, after all.

Then she prepared some watercolour paper for painting on later. She soaked the large, thick sheets in the sink and laid them on flat wooden boards, sticking the edges down with brown gum tape. As the paper dried, it would shrink and tighten, creating a perfectly level surface that was ideal for a watercolour wash.

She kept glancing at the clock and then the door,

willing Francine to come home so she could get it all off her chest. Kali picked up on her jumpiness and walked in circles in the kitchen, getting underfoot and looking concerned. Eventually Penny had to go into the back garden and play fetch for a while, and it was more for Penny's own sake than Kali's.

When she returned to the kitchen, she saw on her phone that she had missed a call from Drew, and she felt even more annoyed. She called him back right away but it went to voicemail. She tried to leave a message but it ended up being a garbled "Yeah hi, I was in the garden sorry, call me, if you can, whenever, hope you're all right."

She hadn't seen Drew for a while. He had been so busy and she was starting to realise that his priority was his work. She didn't want to be second fiddle to anyone.

Yet all through her working life, she hadn't put her own relationships first. Men had had to fit around her schedule, and mostly, they grew tired of waiting for commitment, and drifted away. Now the boot was on the other foot, and she didn't particularly like it.

I have got to make an effort if this is important to me, she thought, *but he has to meet me halfway on this. But I need to tell him so.*

Penny started chopping the vegetables for the stew, and she still felt out of sorts.

So much for my gentle early retirement, she thought. *Are people designed to operate at a certain level of stress? Am I making all this hassle up, just for my brain to have something to fret about?*

* * * *

Francine didn't return to the cottage until early evening. She bounced into the kitchen, and declared that the smell of the stew was "the finest thing I have ever smelled!"

"I thought we might have it with some fresh bread," Penny said. "Are you ready to eat?"

"You don't need to cook for me," Francine said, taking a seat at the table expectantly.

"While you're a guest in my house, I will," Penny said. "But you can get up and lay the table. You know where the cutlery is."

"Of course!" If Francine noticed Penny's snippy tone, she gave no sign of it. She leaped to her feet and began to dig around in the drawers. "I'll butter the bread, too, if you want."

"Sure. That would be helpful."

They moved around the room in a careful dance, and Francine chattered about her day. It wasn't until they had sat down to eat that Francine paused for long enough that Penny could say, "Er, Francine, so what *are* your plans?"

"Tonight? I don't think there's anything on telly. Do you want to go out to the cinema?"

"No, I didn't mean tonight. You've been here a week or so, now. Actually, two weeks. Have you really given up your job in London?"

"I have. My heart hadn't been in it for a while. Um ..." She tailed off and stirred her spoon around the bowl. "This stew is ace, by the way. Really good. Um. And when you left London, I realised that we all get stuck in the same old routines just out of habit, you know? Work wasn't going as well as it could have done. You know ... And I did some soul searching and I picked up some amazing books and I started to learn about how we can ask the universe for what we want and as long as our intentions are good, we'll get what we ask for!"

"I don't believe that for one minute. I spent my entire teenage years asking to be two inches taller. The universe completely ignored me."

Francine waved a hunk of bread in the air. "Oh, we don't always get exactly what we think we want but we do always get what we need! Anyway it's just the start of this journey for me. You prompted me to begin it. Who knows where I'll end up?"

Penny swallowed her sarcastic reply of "far away from here, and soon." Instead, she said, "I am delighted for you, but you can't just jump into decisions like this. I planned my retirement and my move for ages. I carefully considered where I was going to live, and how my budget would stretch."

Francine looked quizzical, her narrow eyes even thinner as she pondered. "I thought you came up here because you were trying to reconnect with your impulsive, freer younger self?"

"Well, yes. But in a calm and rational way."

"But—"

Penny knew that Francine's argument would probably be justified, and she was grateful when someone knocked at the front door. Kali launched herself from her spot under the table. She'd been hoping for stray crumbs to fall, but the potential excitement of a visitor trumped even the pull of food, and she hurled herself at the front door, her tail wagging so much that her hindquarters were making circles.

"Back! Sit."

If Kali was able to sit quietly while Penny opened the door, she would be rewarded by being allowed to greet the visitor. Kali knew this, but her impulse control was a work in progress. She managed to stay in the sit position for about four seconds before the sight of Cath was too much for her, and she lunged past Penny.

"Oh, gerroffme," Cath laughed as she tickled Kali's ears.

"She thinks her name is 'gerroffme' because that's what everyone says when they see her. Come on through. We're just finishing our dinner."

"Tea."

"Dinner. I still have my southern standards. I'll make you a cup of tea, though."

"Don't worry. You finish up, and I'll get the kettle on myself," Cath said. "Ah – hi, there."

"Francine, this is Cath. Cath, Francine."

Francine grinned brightly. "You're the police woman! I've heard about you. It's so nice to see you."

"I'm a detective constable," Cath said.

Francine didn't register the correction. She got to her feet and scooped up a tray from the worktop. "I'll take my dinner through to the other room and let you two chat," she said. "I'm under Penny's feet far too much as it is."

She disappeared, and the door shut firmly behind her. Cath busied herself at the sink while Penny finished her stew. She hadn't expected Francine to be so understanding. She thought she'd be prising the woman out of the conversation.

Unless she was listening at the door.

But she dismissed the thought. Francine was in-your-face honest. She wouldn't hide behind doors.

Unlike Penny. She acknowledged that in many respects, Francine was annoying her just because she was the sort of nice person that Penny thought she herself *ought* to be … but wasn't.

"What's up?" Cath said. "You're miles away. I thought you'd be wall to wall questions at me."

"Yeah. Sorry. Just…" Penny nodded in the direction Francine had gone. "You know."

"She seems perfectly nice," Cath said in a low voice.

"She is. But she won't *go*."

Cath flared her nostrils. Penny knew that she, like the anonymous man in the Sculpture Trail meeting, thought she ought to simply tell Francine to leave. Cath was a capable and solid mother of two and had a demanding career; she couldn't run her life and her household effectively if she pranced around, avoiding issues, like Penny did.

"Right," said Penny decisively. She stood up.

"You're going to tell her right now?"

"No, I'm going to put my bowl in the sink and then slice up a cake."

"Oh, right. Shop-bought or…"

"Don't panic," Penny assured her. "I didn't try to make it. I do learn from my mistakes. I bought it."

"Great. Okay, so I do have stuff to tell you," Cath went on. "Our science folks are really on something at the moment. Maybe they don't have a lot else to do in the lab. I imagine when they're bored, they make up stink bombs and stuff. I would. Anyway, so they came back with the preliminary results for Alec Goodwin's death."

"Don't leave me hanging! Murder?"

Cath sighed. "Maybe and maybe not. He died of poisoning."

"Most poisonings are accidents, aren't they? I would have thought it's a tricky way to kill someone. If you want to be absolutely sure that someone's dead, there are more effective ways."

"You've thought too much about that," Cath said.

"Yeah. I have. I didn't always get on with my work colleagues."

Cath grinned. "Okay. I will confess that sometimes, when I'm interviewing a suspect and they admit to doing some crime or another, that I often think 'I would have done that differently…'"

Penny sat back in her chair. "What poisoned him? Do you know that yet?"

"The boffins need to grow stuff in dishes, I think, before they will confirm anything. I don't know why. They did say it looked like an alkaloid of some kind, a bitter substance, and there was a lot of it. They suggested without being totally certain that it was *unlikely* to be an accident."

"Suicide?"

"Maybe…"

Penny thought for a moment. "No, I don't think so, and I can tell from your face that you don't think so, either. It would be an impractical way to kill yourself."

"And a painful one. I won't give you the details, but he didn't die ... well."

Penny shuddered. "The poor man. Does it sound strange to say that I hope it's a tragic accident? I don't want to think about the sort of person who would do that to another human being, that's all."

"I understand," Cath said. "Don't let it prey on your mind. You don't have to be involved if you don't want to be."

"My information was useful before."

"Yes, but not at the expense of your mental health."

"Thanks." Penny nodded. "More cake. Cake makes everything all right."

"Bring it on."

They had another small slice, and Cath groaned. "I should have said no."

"Let's go for a walk."

"Where?"

"You already know where." Penny opened the door

to the living room. As she suspected, Francine was peacefully sitting at the far end of the room, pointedly not eavesdropping. "Francine, there's some cake in here. Help yourself. We're going for a wander."

"How lovely! Thanks!"

* * * *

"You want to go poking around Alec's house, don't you?" Cath said as they walked through the sultry evening. It seemed like most of Upper Glenfield was out on the streets, and the persistent hot weather was making tempers fray. They could hear arguments as well as laughter, and the lingering smell of barbecues and the slow cremation of sausages plagued them all the way out of town.

"I do," Penny admitted. "Come on, please, can I? I didn't get to look around before."

"We'll see who's on duty down there. If it's PC Patel, please don't terrorise him."

"He can handle himself, I'm sure."

"He's scared of you," Cath said.

Penny was quietly pleased, but she said, "Sorry. I don't

mean to terrify anyone. It just happens."

It wouldn't be dark for another two hours yet. They walked on, and Cath asked if Penny had unearthed any interesting gossip yet.

"No," Penny said. "Alec Goodwin was such a recluse that everything seems to be mere speculation. Mary from the craft group thought he was strapped for cash and that was why he took on the Sculpture Trail. She also says that 'everyone' says he was murdered, but people do like to say stuff like that."

"Yeah, people can be horrible," Cath said. "They forget it's a real person involved. On the other hand, if he was murdered, someone somewhere will know something and often that's how rumours start. So it's worth keeping your ears open. If something strange keeps getting repeated, we want to know."

"Oh, there's more," Penny said as they grew closer to Alec's house. She could see a police officer standing by the gate. "The town council or whoever it is who are responsible for the Sculpture Trail grant went and asked Ginni to take over from Alec."

"Ginni's not a sculptor, is she?"

"No, I don't think so. And anyway, she said no. Because she thought it should have been Steve."

"Maybe it should have. If you're thinking foul play ..." Cath said.

"...then maybe Ginni is on the list, not her nephew."

Cath ran her hand through her hair and sighed. "I really, really don't want to consider Ginni as a potential murderer. She's a local stalwart."

"I know."

The police officer on duty that night was a tall, rangy woman who waved them through with a grin. Cath led Penny to the front door, and pulled out two pairs of latex gloves from her pocket. "Don't touch a thing," she warned. "But just in case you do, wear these."

"Crikey. The dodgy things that police officers have to keep in their pockets!" Penny said with a laugh.

"These are my home clothes," Cath pointed out. "I've got the gloves because I have messy small boys, pets and a husband who ..."

"I don't want to know any more, thanks."

"Come on, then."

The front door opened into a hallway that ran right

down the centre of the house, from front to back. The floor was tiled and cold. A staircase led up to the rooms above. Cath led her first into the room to the left, which was a general sitting room, with old-fashioned wing-back chairs that were threadbare and uncomfortable-looking.

"No television?" Penny said.

"Nope. Just a big old radio, and lots of books."

The room was lined with shelves and it smelled like old paper. There were, remarkably, no pictures on the walls. It felt bare and unloved.

"Now come and see the kitchen," Cath said. The way she smiled gave Penny a clue that she was in for a surprise, but even forewarned, she was still taken aback when she entered.

"Goodness."

"It's something else, isn't it?" Cath said, grinning with delight.

Penny shook her head and stared around at the shiny white surfaces and pristine gadgets. It was the sort of kitchen that she'd only ever seen in glossy magazines, and occasionally when she'd been to exclusive dinner parties in London, when she was young and easily impressed.

Who was she kidding? She was *still* impressed. She walked around the central island. "He seems to have been a real foodie," she said. "There are things here that I don't even recognise. Is that some kind of fancy coffee percolator, do you think?"

"I reckon so." Cath pointed at the rows of jars and packets. "He looks to have been a real coffee snob."

Penny peered closely at the labels, keeping her hands by her sides. "He didn't just buy these down the mini-market," she said. "These are imports and all sorts."

"You didn't expect a kitchen like this, did you?"

"No, not at all. I'm stunned, to be honest."

Penny and Cath walked slowly around. She was itching to pick things up but she had to be content with studying things as closely as she could. "There's a label on this packet of coffee with the price only in dollars," she said. "Cath, where *did* he buy all this from?"

"He must have got it all off the internet," Cath said.

Penny pursed her lips. "Hmm. So he doesn't have a television but he does have the internet?"

"That's getting more common, isn't it?" Cath said. "When we deal with younger folk now, like at the university in Lincoln, they tend not to have tellies because they can watch whatever they want online."

"Is it upstairs?"

"What?"

"His computer. Because there was nothing in the studio or in the other room and there's nothing in here, is there?"

Cath and Penny considered one another. "Now you mention it … no. We can have a peep upstairs but there was nothing remarkable. I don't remember any kind of computing device being logged, not even a smartphone. But come on, let's get your fresh eyes on it."

But Cath was right. They gazed around the two bedrooms and small bathroom, and Penny saw nothing but the same mess and disregard for housework that was evident in the living room. It was as if the kitchen belonged to someone else entirely.

And crucially, there was no sign of a computer, laptop, tablet or anything.

"Does he have a landline?" Penny asked.

"Yes."

They found a yellowed plastic handset in the hallway.

Once, it had been white, but sunlight had aged it. They traced the cable back to the main socket on the outside wall.

"No kind of modem or router," Cath said.

"There's the public computers in the library, and the sessions that Reg runs at the community centre," Penny said.

"Reg? Not Reg Bailey?"

"The very same. He does these courses for 'silver surfers' now. They're free. He was always into local history, apparently, and he has started up some kind of website."

"That's cool. I'll get someone to pop into all the local libraries and ask them. You use the one here in Glenfield – have you seen Alec there?"

"Never," said Penny. "But he might have travelled out of town."

"He really was an odd one," Cath said. "But what would make someone want to kill him?"

"*If* he was killed," Penny pointed out. They wandered back into the kitchen. It was the only room that didn't feel sad and unloved. "What was it that killed him again? The poison, I mean?"

"They said it was an alkaloid, that it would have tasted

very bitter, and he had had such a large amount of it that they are uncertain that it could have been accidental. It's still possible, though. Or suicide, but as you say, it's a strange way to do yourself in. I think we'll know more when the final results come in."

"I don't really know what an alkaloid is," Penny said. "The opposite of acid? Or am I thinking of alkali? We did that at school but I was sitting near a mean girl called Karen and so I didn't get much work done in chemistry because she was always passing me nasty notes."

"Why did you read them if they were nasty?"

"I don't know. Because I was a teenage girl? Who knows why we do what we do."

Cath shook her head and rolled her eyes. "I am glad I've had boys. They are so much easier. Anyway, the boffins did explain alkaloids to me. They are mostly from plants, and fungi and stuff. That's why we considered accidental overdose, you see."

"Ahh. He's obviously a foodie, so eating the wrong sort of mushrooms, that sort of thing?"

"Exactly."

Penny stared again at the coffee. "Coffee is bitter," she

said, slowly, as she felt her way along the thought process. "If you wanted to poison someone with a bitter-tasting thing, you'd hide it in something that was also bitter…"

Cath nodded. "Yeah …"

"But, as you say, until we know more …"

"Yup. It's all speculation. Come on, let's get going. There's still some cake left at your house, and I've heard that it can go mouldy very quickly in this weather. Like, within minutes. Let's not take the risk."

"You're right. We had better get back."

* * * *

Francine looked surprised that Cath came back into the house when they returned. All three sat in the kitchen, having another cup of tea, until Francine pointedly yawned and took herself off to bed. Cath left not long after that.

Penny cleared away the plates, and took Kali outside for her regular night time sniff-the-plants routine.

Did Francine's bubbly exterior mask some other problems? Penny realised that she had been so caught up in her own feelings that she'd never actually bothered to ask. She was increasingly sure that there was something else going on.

She leaned on the doorframe and stared up at the myriad stars above. Tomorrow, she resolved she'd ask. She'd be a better person.

Starting tomorrow.

CHAPTER FIVE

Penny was startled awake by her mobile phone ringing, and she knew it was impossibly early because usually Kali was staring at her by seven in the morning, trying to wake Penny by the power of her glare. She groped for her phone and didn't recognise the caller's number.

She answered it anyway. Her parents were getting on in age now, and their jet-setting lifestyle of endless cruises and city breaks couldn't last forever. If the call turned out to merely be a telemarketer, however, they were going to regret disturbing her this early in the morning.

It was someone else; and it was someone entirely unexpected.

"Penelope? It's Ariadne. Are you there? Is this still your number? Er …"

Penny sat up straight and rubbed her eyes with her free

hand. She hadn't heard her younger sister's voice for two years.

"Penelope?" the voice said again. "I'm sorry ... who am I talking to?"

"Hi. Yeah, this is Penny. Ariadne ..."

"Oh, thank goodness! Penelope ... I'm sorry to ring so early."

"Is everything okay with mum and dad?" Penny's adrenaline was on overdrive straight away.

"Yes, as far as I know. Sorry. Yes. This isn't an emergency, really. I just wanted to say ... hello. That's all. It's been too long since we've spoken. And I couldn't let that carry on, you know?"

"Right." Penny realised that Kali was staring at her in concern, and she patted the bed beside her. She took a deep breath. "It's okay," she whispered to the dog. "Come on up ... good girl."

"Am I disturbing you? Do you have someone there?"

"Just Kali. It's okay. Let me move over for her."

"Oh! Penelope! I ... I never realised ..."

"She's my dog."

"Of course. Oh. Right."

There was a silence, and Penny knew that she was

expected to ask about Ariadne's husband and children. She remembered the previous night's vow to be a nicer person, and so through gritted teeth, she said, "And is everything okay with you and yours?"

"Mmm. Owen's still, well, you know. He's just the same as always. Everyone's finding it hard with jobs, though, aren't they? It's not just him. Oh, Star was eighteen last week."

The accusation fell like lead. Penny hadn't sent a card. "Oh," she said, and then in a rush, "I'm sorry. I am." It wasn't the kid's fault, was it? "I should have sent something," she admitted. "I *am* sorry. How are the others?"

"Destiny's looking forward to being able to leave school. It was never her thing. She's too much like her dad. Wolf, on the other hand, is top in everything. I don't know where he gets it from!" Ariadne laughed, and to Penny's ears it sounded false and brittle.

There must be another reason for Ariadne to call her. They had never been close sisters, with eleven years between them. "Are you happy, Ariadne?" Penny asked, impulsively. "Is something wrong?"

It was not the right thing to ask. Ariadne shut down

immediately. "I've got a family and I've got love," she said. "I was calling to see if *you* were all right. Are you still single?"

"Mostly," she countered, "as is my choice. I didn't mean—"

"You did mean," Ariadne said. "London makes everyone mean."

"I don't live in London any longer. I'm in Lincolnshire."

"When?"

"Ah. Three months ago, or so."

"I didn't know." And this time the accusatory silence cut into Penny because she knew she should have told Ariadne. After all, she only lived about an hour away, over the county border in Leicestershire.

"I thought mum and dad would have told you," Penny said.

"They probably assumed it would be down to you. Ah, one minute—" Ariadne's voice became muffled, and Penny heard her swear. Suddenly Ariadne said, "Look, have fun in Lincolnshire. I'm glad to hear you're all right. Gotta go—"

And that was it. The phone beeped and the static dial tone came on.

Penny put the phone back on the nightstand and absently stroked Kali's head and shoulders. Why would you call before even seven in the morning?

When you didn't want to be overheard.

Why call someone you had only ever argued with?

When you had no one else left to call.

Penny felt heavy and sad as she got out of bed, stretched, and made her way to the bathroom to start the morning.

* * * *

"No," she told her own reflection. "I am not a moping-around sort of woman."

"No, you're not," said Francine, appearing on the landing and speaking through the slightly-open bathroom door. "You're someone who gets things done. Hey, do you remember when we were in Sydney, and we hired that crane but it got stolen in the night and those kids went on a joyride and we were on the news and everything?"

Penny spun around. "Er..."

"Because the executive producer had that massive meltdown and you stepped in, even though you were only an assistant back then, and you handled the television interview even though you'd just had that terrible haircut and everything?"

It was hardly the worst experience I've ever had, Penny thought. But it was one of the defining moments in her early career. "I remember."

"You didn't mope around then, even when the exec came and bawled you out for overstepping the mark and exceeding your authority."

"Well. No, I didn't mope. But what else was there to do?"

"Exactly," Francine said in triumph, as if she had just unfurled a great insight for Penny and was now simply awaiting her gratitude.

"Well, quite. Thank you."

"You're welcome. Shall we go out for a walk?"

She had to say yes. "Okay."

* * * *

They took the dog and it gave them something to talk about. Francine was also reminiscing about the past, and sharing some tales about mutual friends and colleagues that

Penny hadn't heard before, or had forgotten about.

They laughed and they giggled.

It was fun.

By the time they got back, at midday, Penny felt a lot better. In a bid to continue being a "nicer person" she impulsively grabbed her phone and called Drew, taking the conversation out into the back garden while Francine settled in the living room with a book.

As usual, he was dashing from place to place. "I've just finished a session up at Acorns," he said apologetically, referring to the special school for children with behavioural problems. "I'm shattered. Those kids have enough energy to power a city. I don't know how the teachers do it all day. And I've got half an hour before I have to be back at the hotel to take a party of accountants out this afternoon. I'm supposed to teach them how to light fires."

"Why do accountants need to learn that?"

"To burn the evidence? I don't know. I was told this department needs to work as a team. I suppose that means that they've been stealing each other's milk from the office kitchen."

"Drew ... have you any free time coming up?"

There was a pause. She wondered if she was being too forward. Then she shrugged. If he couldn't handle that, she wasn't going to pretend to be something else.

In spite of her pretended indifference, she was relieved when he laughed. "I have. Tomorrow afternoon, after three … do you want to do anything in particular?"

"Not really. I just fancy getting out and walking somewhere."

"I'll call by. I miss seeing Kali, anyway."

"How rude!"

"Gotta go," he said, and she could hear him still laughing as he hung up.

* * * *

"Call by." Penny rolled her eyes at herself as she stared at the various items of clothing she had scattered on her bed. "Call by," that's what he'd said. There was no use dressing up for someone who was just "calling by," right?

But the weather was hot and humid and muggy, and she'd recently had her hair bleached out to blonde with some peacock-blue stripes, which were already fading to a disappointing green. It was the sort of summer weather that did prompt you to change your clothes a few times a day, and stay permanently under a cold shower if it were at all possible.

So Penny slipped out of her khaki shorts and t-shirt, and into a floaty sun dress that had a nipped-in waist and a vintage feel to the way it flared out above her knees.

Drew was right on time, and she invited him in to try some sorbet she'd bought, but he suggested they go for a drive. With the windows open, he said, it would be more pleasant than staying still anywhere, and she agreed.

They chatted about inconsequential things, and it was lovely. He spoke about his various new jobs, especially about the manager of the Arches Hotel and Conference Centre, Brian, who was being very supportive.

Or, demanding, was another way of looking at it.

"I've got more work than I can handle at the moment," Drew said ruefully, his arm resting on the rolled-down window as they took a curving and rural route south of Upper Glenfield. "But I keep saying yes, just in case it all dries up and I end up starving …"

Penny laughed. She knew that feeling well.

On they went, with Penny sharing stories of her life behind the scenes in television, and Drew telling her about the local hero, Hereward the Saxon, whose ghost was apparently still sighted in the woods above a small town called Bourne. He pulled into the car parking area, and they wandered out along a path that was cool and shady.

"There's some that call him Hereward the Wake," Drew said as they pottered along.

"Ah! I have heard of him," she said.

"Well, the thing is, the Wake family were Normans, and it was Normans that he was fighting. So they took his lands and everything, and it's victors that write history, so by calling him 'the Wake' when they wrote about it, they could somehow claim legitimacy."

"Sneaky."

"I reckon he's the first English freedom fighter. Except when you look at being 'English' and you look at all the different peoples that have invaded over the years – Normans included – we're a bunch of mongrels, really."

"Anyway, he didn't win, did he?" Penny said. "The Normans took over."

"For a while, I suppose, until we assimilated them like

we do to everyone. It's quite cool, actually, don't you think?"

Penny smiled at Drew's passion. "Yes, I suppose it is. Was he defeated in battle, like a true hero?"

"It's a bit bizarre, actually. The story goes that he was holed up on the Fens. I think it was on the Isle of Ely. The Normans were attacking and they had a witch in a tower that they pushed towards the Isle, chanting and casting spells."

Penny laughed out loud. "No way."

"It's the story. Who knows? Anyway the witch wasn't much use but one of the monks on the Isle was treacherous, and betrayed them, leading the Normans in to where they were hiding. Hereward escaped … or so they say."

Penny grinned. "A witch in a tower. I can't imagine a bunch of armed men finding that scary."

"But it's all a matter of perception," Drew said. "Look at it in context. What about this Alec Goodwin?"

"How do you mean?"

"Well," he said. "I know you'll be listening out for information. But everyone has an opinion and it's all filtered through what they already think they know about artists, and people who want to be reclusive, and all that sort of thing. I don't we ever see anything as it truly is."

"Gosh, that's philosophical."

He laughed, then, and picked up his pace. "I know. I'm sorry. I'm working so hard these days that sometimes my thoughts go off on very mad tangents. Wait – hush." He put out a hand and stopped her, and dropped his voice to a whisper as he came to a sudden stop. "Look up there."

It was a herd of deer, passing through the trees and bushes. "What are they?" she said in a low voice. "And don't just say 'deer'."

"Fallow," he replied. "Not native. They were introduced by the Normans, too, as it happens. Now they are some of the most common in the UK."

"Wow. Beautiful," she whispered as the last few darted past.

"Tasty, too," he said, and she hit him hard on the arm. "Ow! Joking."

"Not funny."

He shot a sideways glance at her, and appeared to be about to speak. She glared.

He shrugged, and they carried on.

CHAPTER SIX

Drew dropped her off in the late afternoon and she felt relaxed and at ease after spending a few hours in his easy company.

That evening, Francine insisted on ordering take-away food. There was one fish and chip shop in the town, and they had recently started a home delivery service. Their cod and chips, twice, were duly delivered, wrapped up in paper. Penny tipped the young lad on the moped quite generously, which she knew would ensure she always had prompt service in the future.

"Messy?" Francine asked as they unwrapped the food in the kitchen. Penny recoiled as the sting of vinegar and salt fumes hit her eyes and made them water.

"Messy," she agreed.

It was a code they both remembered from when they'd

travelled together, two young members of large production crews. It meant bare, basic food, enjoyed from the wrappers rather than from plates, eaten off the knees while sitting on walls or in parks. They took two trays and went through to the living room, and Kali was relegated to a spot on the carpet to watch them as they ate with their fingers.

"Come on, Francine," Penny said, not looking at her friend. It was now or never. She concentrated on dipping her chips in the blob of ketchup she'd put at the side of the unfurled paper. "Tell me why you're here. Why you're *really* here. Did something go horribly wrong in London?"

"Not at all!" Francine chirped. Her voice was light and amused. Penny couldn't imagine Francine lying to her, so she had to assume she wasn't hiding anything. Not exactly lying, perhaps, but maybe she just wasn't saying everything.

"I don't understand this manifesting one's destiny rubbish, either," Penny said, hoping a sideways change of topic would help.

"You don't have to understand it. I don't understand gravity, but it works, right?"

"Gravity is science."

"If it works for me, though, then why not?"

Penny sighed. "But what if it's all made up nonsense?" She truly believed it was.

"Again, does it matter, if it gives me a focus?" Francine said.

"I suppose not."

"Look," Francine said. "There's more than one way to live a life. There's more than one way to understand life. There's more than one way to do anything."

The words stuck in Penny's head and she couldn't shake them free. It obviously meant something to her subconscious so she filed it away, and said, with a defeated air, "Do you fancy a cup of tea with this?"

"Ooh, yes please. Thank you."

As Penny stood up, Francine spoke again. Her voice was low. "And thank you for letting me stay. I know you didn't expect me to turn up. I ... haven't been totally honest with you. The reason I came here was ... well, it's hard, but things weren't going well at work."

Penny cocked her head on one side. Just as she had suspected, though she was genuinely shocked that Francine had said she'd not been honest. She asked, with concern, "What happened?"

Francine looked sad, briefly. She gabbled, "Oh, just some nasty talk, and I realised I was fed up of it. Life's too short, hey? Anyway. Weren't you making some tea?"

It was a clear signal that the conversation was over. Penny was intrigued but knew she should not press it.

Not yet.

And maybe it was not time to ask Francine to leave.

* * * *

Penny went to bed and dreamed, and when she woke up on Thursday morning, she felt more clear in her purpose.

She'd dreamed about Reg Bailey, of all people. The elderly gentleman was an old-school type, always seen in a neat blazer and well-pressed chinos. He believed in politeness, writing thank-you letters, and public floggings for people who dropped litter.

There was more than one way to do something, Francine had told her. It reminded her of Alec and his lack of computer. Penny and Cath had talked about how he'd got online, and Penny realised that she had to go and talk to Reg.

It wasn't a message from the universe, she knew. She thought if she mentioned it to Francine, she'd get a long explanation about how the universe knew what she needed. It was just her own brain reminding her to get on with things and stop floating around in a mood.

She dressed in her favourite clothes. Her fitted tunic made her feel slim, and her bright blue linen trousers were floaty and comfortable in the heat. She had just finished her breakfast when Francine appeared in the kitchen.

"You look nice."

"Thank you. I'm off out, investigating. It is about time I got started."

"Oh! That's good. I'll take Kali for a walk, shall I?"

"No, it's all right," Penny said, and Francine's face fell.

"I want to help," Francine insisted. "And I want to bond more with Kali. Please let me help. It's my way of saying thanks for letting me stay and everything."

So it was out of Penny's hands, and she felt a pang as she watched Kali happily trot off with Francine.

But she had things to do, and it clearly did Francine some good, and it was going to help Penny. She stepped out into town and walked with a swinging, decisive step.

She went first to the tiny satellite library in Upper Glenfield. She usually visited the larger one in Lincoln for her books, but the small local library was open four mornings a week and had two computers for general public use. It was staffed by a slender and efficient young woman with enormous glasses and a mass of soft, fuzzy, mousey-blonde hair.

"Hi! I wonder if you can help me."

"Sure. What are you looking for?"

"Not a book, as such. But information, yes. Um, do you know that sculptor, Alec Goodwin?"

The librarian made a suitably sad face. "I had heard of him, because he died recently, didn't he?"

"Yes, that's right. I wondered if he ever used the library here. Specifically, did he come in to use the computers?"

The librarian shook her head. "The police came in and asked me the same thing. No, he didn't, as far as I know. I know the names of all my regulars."

"Thank you."

Penny left the library and someone seemed to have turned up the heat outside while she'd been talking in the cool interior. Lincolnshire in the summer was a furnace, and she wasn't used to it. She pulled her shades out of her tote bag and paused on the pavement. She knew where Reg lived. He had a large and detached house along Cuthbert Road, which was a select and exclusive residential area to the south of Glenfield. First, though, she made her way to the mini-market, and checked out the noticeboard.

She was looking for the posters about the "Silver Surfer Classes" that he was involved with. She didn't really know him well enough to simply turn up on his doorstep to ask some questions. She'd tried that before, more than once, and it had never ended well. She was learning that she had to be a little more sensitive with her approach.

There it was – an A4 sheet of paper with more use of clip-art and word art than she'd seen for many years. "You're not too old to get online!" the blocky text headline in a flag-waving shape proclaimed. "Weekday mornings, 9am to 10am, Community Centre."

Penny frowned. She couldn't remember even seeing any computers at the community centre, and when she checked her watch, it was already a quarter past ten.

But it was worth a shot. She turned around, and briskly made her way through town and down the road that led out to the small community centre.

* * * *

And she was in luck. When she reached the long, low building, there was an old but immaculate Jaguar parked outside, in flagrant defiance of the yellow lines on the road. A dapper figure in a white suit was loading boxes into the boot of the car.

She hailed him as she approached. "Good morning, Mr Bailey!"

He turned and smiled, and raised one hand cordially. "Ahh, Miss May. How lovely to see you. Are you well?"

"I am, thanks. Yourself?"

"Mustn't grumble. I could do with a little less heat and a little more rain for my roses, but all in all, what a glorious summer we're having."

"Yes, lovely."

He looked at her with a hint of wariness. The last time they'd met, it had been under the sobering circumstances of another man's death, and Reg Bailey had had to face some uncomfortable family secrets. She didn't want to rake over those things, and she could tell that neither did he.

"I've come to ask you about Alec Goodwin," she said, wanting him to know straight away what her intentions were.

He stilled, and raised one grey eyebrow. "Me? Are you still meddling in things you ought not meddle in?"

"Yes, I am. Again."

He barked out a short laugh. "Honest, aren't you? Mr Goodwin was a recluse. No one knows anything about the poor man. It is the definition, one might say, of a recluse. And now he's gone, and what a tragedy." But even Reg couldn't keep the curiosity wholly at bay. "So was he murdered, then?"

"It's not been established yet," she said. "But I've been to his house, and there was something odd about it."

"He's an artist," Reg said scornfully. No doubt he wouldn't be surprised to learn that Alec had had a cellar kitted out with strange and dubious furniture, stuffed crocodiles and shrunken heads.

"Well, yes, but he also seemed to be really, *really* into fine coffee."

Reg relaxed and brushed his hands together. He nodded. "Come and help me carry the last few laptops out, if you will."

She followed him into the pleasantly cool interior. "Laptops."

"That's what I said."

"So you teach people to get online?"

"I do." He smiled very proudly. "And yes, Alec sought me out for some help. He didn't come to these sessions, though. He had no patience for being near other people. He would come to my house from time to time, and I set him up with some online accounts and showed him how to buy things. I know he liked ordering fancy foods and drink. And you are quite correct. He did love his coffee."

Reg passed her two laptops and a case full of leads and power cables, and she followed him back out to his car, where she stood while he arranged things in the boot.

"When was the last time you saw him?" she asked.

"I knew that was your next question. And it did stick in my mind as being a little strange. He turned up at my house last Friday, just out of the blue. He never usually does that. And he asked me to do some research."

Reg slammed the boot shut, and made his way back into the hall. She followed. Reg had a way of moving around that made you feel as if you had to obey him. He held the door open for her, and she passed by him with a dignified nod, reserving her feminist rant for another, more appropriate time.

"Research about what?" Penny asked. She perched on a table while he went around the hall, tidying up the chairs and picking up stray pens and paper.

"I have been interested in local history for many years," Reg told her. "I am, if I may say, something of an expert. I often give talks at the Women's Institute. I had thought that interest in our heritage was sadly dying, and I must confess I'd been quite sad about the whole thing."

She nodded.

"However!" he continued with a flourish. "However! The internet has revitalised it. I learned a little about computers, and started getting online, and realised that what this town really needed was a local history website! You may have seen it…?"

She had not, and she hadn't realised one existed. "No, I'm afraid I haven't, but I shall be sure to look it up."

"One moment." He grabbed a scrap of paper and wrote a long and clumsy website address on it for her. She saw immediately why she hadn't heard of it. It wasn't something simple and useful like "Glenfield.co.uk" or whatever, although that was probably already taken by a company with a similar name. She pocketed the slip of paper with her thanks.

"And as word has spread of my researching prowess," Reg said, "it was to me that Alec came when he wanted to find out about two people from his past."

"Old friends?"

"I'm not entirely sure. I don't recollect the reason, and I am certainly not the sort of man who'd pry."

"Can you remember the names of them?"

He frowned, as if asking him to recall them was in itself an act of prying, but eventually he said, "Yes, because I had to have him spell out Carl with a c not a k. Carl and Amanda Fredericks."

"Mr Bailey, this might be really important," Penny said. "I think the police will want to know."

"I really don't think I ought to bother them."

She guessed he was also the sort of person who wouldn't bother their doctor with anything less than actual bubonic plague. "Please do tell them. I'm going to be honest with you – I'm going to mention it to Cath Pritchard."

"I know. Nothing I say to you is sacred." He smiled a little so that she understood he wasn't being nasty.

"Thank you. If you remember anything else, such as *why* he wanted to find out about them, will you let me – or Cath – know?"

"Of course. I know some people consider you to be a dreadful interferer, and I did think that myself, when we met under those … difficult … circumstances. But on reflection I think that you're acting out of a fine civic nature and more people ought to be involved in their community. There are some real locals who don't get as involved as you do!"

So she wasn't a "real" local. She shook her head and smiled. "I'm also really nosey," she pointed out.

He took her elbow proprietorially and steered her back out into the sunlight. "I do remember something about that Carl Fredericks chap. He runs a bulb business out east, out on the Fens. It was lovely chatting with you, Miss May. Take care."

"And you. Thank you again!" She really meant it. She could put up with his well-meaning chivalry because now she had some information to follow up.

And he was a charming man, she acknowledged. She stood on the pavement and watched the elegant car cruise away. *Some* men, she thought pointedly, could do well to learn from him.

She turned for home, but went via the town centre. She had one more appointment to make.

CHAPTER SEVEN

"I was pleased you could fit me in this afternoon," Penny told Agatha later that day as she settled into the chair.

The hairdresser stood behind Penny, but they talked by looking in the mirror. Agatha ran her fingers through Penny's short hair. "I was surprised to see you back so soon. Don't you like the blue streaks?"

"I love them," Penny said, and in truth there was little reason for her to be back at the salon. However, she wanted gossip. "But I'm a bit alarmed by the greenish tint. And I just felt it needed shortening at the back and the sides need more shape. It's grown so quickly."

Agatha pulled the strands at the back. "I warned you about the green," she said ruefully.

"I know. It's fine. But the shape …?"

"I'll give you a trim," Agatha said. "How's that sound, eh?"

"Brilliant, thank you."

Agatha mentioned the weather, remarked upon Penny's shoes, and asked after her dog. Those formalities concluded within a matter of minutes and she was able to launch into the meaty stuff: talking about Alec Goodwin.

"You're all hand in nest with the police," she said. "So how did he die, eh? I won't tell a soul! I promise."

Penny smiled at the mixed up phrase, thinking she had to remember that to tell to Francine. She said, "He was poisoned but it *could* have been an accident. Unless you've heard anything definitely different…"

"Everyone says he was murdered!"

"By whom, though? Who would want to kill him?"

"I don't know. But I can tell you this: that Steve has some questions to answer now, doesn't he?"

"What about?"

"Well now!" Agatha said explosively. "He's agreed to take over the Sculpture Trail!"

"I bet his aunt Ginni is pleased."

"That's just the thing," Agatha said. She flashed the scissors close to Penny's ear. "She won't talk to anyone about it. She's gone into a proper munk, she has."

"A what?"

"A strop, a mood. You know. She's right mardy."

"I see. I think. But why?"

"She still seems to be angry that they hadn't given it to Steve in the first place. Though why she is so set on helping that good-for-nothing, I don't know."

"He's fresh out of university," Penny protested. "I loafed about and did nothing for months when I graduated. I think I thought that the world would come knocking on my door to offer me my dream job."

"Did it, eh?"

"No, of course not. But the point is, that someone in their early twenties, well, most of them, look like good-for-nothings." Steve hadn't made a great impression on her when she'd seen him, but she could still forgive a little youthful lackadaisical attitude.

Agatha sniffed. "That length all right for you, there?"

"Yes, thanks." Penny nodded and Agatha frowned.

"Stay still!"

"Sorry. Anyway, can you tell me why Steve is staying with Ginni and not his actual parents? Who are they? Where do they live?"

Agatha shook her head sadly, as if everyone else knew. "Oh, it's nothing sinister. Let me see. His mum and dad live up on that council estate a mile north of here. Do you know where I mean? On the road to Lincoln, there's that bunch of houses on the left, all grey and blocky. I think it used to be linked to an RAF base because they look like forces houses. Anyway, it's social housing now."

"What's the relationship?"

"Ginni's sister Kate married a chap called Andy. They're good people, you know. I like them. But Andy's always in and out of work. I don't know what it is. He is just one of them as cannot hold down a job. Some folks call him rough but he's a decent man."

"What about Ginni? She lives alone, right? I mean, apart from Steve, now."

"Oh! Ginni's had her share."

"Of …?"

"Men," Agatha said darkly. "She's divorced now. Her daughter lives in Manchester and her husband is probably hiding in Borneo or something."

"Is she really someone who holds a grudge that much? I'm surprised."

"Oh, eh! Is she ever? She's so beholden to what she thinks is right – and by that I mean, she always thinks *she's* right – that she doesn't change her mind very well."

"But I still don't understand why Steve is living with her and not his parents."

Agatha shrugged and picked up a misting spray from the wheeled trolley next to her. "I think most kids out of college don't want to go live with their mum and dad again, do they, eh?"

It was probably that simple. *The problem with looking for clues and hints*, Penny thought, *is that you get to thinking that everything is a clue. Perception, remember.* She took a step back, mentally. "Yeah, you're right," she said.

"How's the hair?"

"It's great," Penny said with a grin.

"I hardly touched it. You only came in for the gossip."

"No, no, no!"

But their eyes met in the mirror, and Penny realised she was pinking just a little around her cheeks.

"Yes," she said, crestfallen.

CHAPTER EIGHT

Francine disappeared off on Friday morning for a walk with Kali before Penny had even got out of bed. She left a note on the kitchen table: "It's so hot and I couldn't sleep so I thought I'd be useful and take Kali out."

She means well, Penny thought. But Penny was feeling increasingly excluded from her relationship with her dog. She'd always dismissed pet lovers' talk of "bonding" as sentimental nonsense. Now, she found it to be a strange and true feeling. She had even looked it up, worried that she was one step away from becoming a "mad dog lady" and found a reassuringly scientific article which claimed that dogs and their owners produced certain feel-good hormones when they looked at one another.

If it was science, it was easier to accept. She didn't follow the links in case it turned out to be cleverly disguised bunkum. She *wanted* to believe.

Like Francine and her "manifesting her destiny."

Penny pushed it out of her mind. She had a job to do, she reminded herself. She sat at the kitchen table and put the radio on low as background company. The house felt curiously empty. She flipped open her laptop and started to search online for Carl Fredericks, using the information Reg had given her to narrow it down.

And there he was. *Fredericks' Bulb Growers* was a horticultural business some twenty miles east, out on the flat fenlands. They had a small and basic website, all square edges and misaligned boxes, and the company seemed to cater to the wholesale trade. She scrolled through pages of daffodils and tulips and irises. There was a bare "About Us" page with a blurred photo of the owner, Carl Fredericks. He looked to be in his fifties, but she couldn't be sure how old the photograph was.

She couldn't find much else about him. If he was on social media, he was pretty private: no one with the same name had a similar profile picture. She had a quick check of some professional networks but nothing came up.

She didn't see much point in digging further, but she

called Cath to fill her in on what she had learned so far.

"Hey there!" Cath said, answering on the second ring. "I was just going to call you."

"Have you got news?"

"The lab says that Alec had ingested an alkaloid poison in a level that was very, very unlikely to have been an accident."

"Murder, then?"

"There are no signs that point to suicide. Yes, at this stage, we are now considering it a murder investigation."

"Oh." She paused, and spared a thought for the dead man. "But who? Have you found any family yet?" She hated the idea that he might be alone and unloved.

"We haven't, no. He was never married, never active socially, nothing. He was sixty years old and he'd lived alone in Upper Glenfield, in that house, for a good twenty years or so."

"Right. Do you have any suspects?"

"We were rather hoping you'd have something for us," Cath said. "I'm on my way down later. Do you want to meet at Alec's house?"

"Sure. Name the time."

* * * *

Penny went on foot. When she reached the driveway entrance to Alec's house, Cath was standing by the blue and white tape, her phone held to her ear.

"Of course," she was saying. "That sounds great. I can come to yours, Mr Bailey. I'm in Glenfield right now, not far away ... yes, that's right. Oh, okay ... you don't have to ..."

The phone call tailed off and Cath shoved the phone into her smart jacket pocket. "Reg Bailey does like his own way, doesn't he? I wish he wouldn't call me a 'lady police woman.' I know he's polite, but it makes me feel I ought to be wearing more pink."

"That's a terrible thought."

"What, me in pink?"

"No, you being considered a lady."

Cath looked as if she were about to make a rude hand gesture at Penny, but she thought better of it. "Anyway. Hi, nice to see you too. So, Reg has some information, apparently, and he's on his way down here to show me."

Penny felt a frisson of excitement at being in the right place at the right time. They didn't have long to wait, and while they stood by the cordon, Penny filled Cath in on the stuff she'd learned about Alec's online activities, which felt woefully little.

"Hmm. I had Steve pegged as a suspect," Cath said, "but this Carl chap sounds worth looking into."

"We might be in luck, then. Here comes Reg."

The Jaguar purred to a stop, and Reg emerged, a vision of dapper Englishness. He even wore a white hat, which he tipped in their direction. "Good afternoon, ladies."

"Hi, Mr Bailey." Penny thought it was so typical of dealing with him that she called him "Reg" in her head and "Mr Bailey" to his face.

Cath was obviously of the same mind. "Hello, Mr Bailey. Thank you for coming down."

He was clutching a sheaf of papers and he fanned himself with them. Cath glanced at the police officer on guard, who nodded.

"Come on, we'll get out of the heat."

"You can't go in the kitchen," the officer said. "Boris will bite your arm off if you go in there. You know what he's like."

"Of course. We'll be in the studio at the back."

Penny and Reg followed Cath around. Penny hung back, trying to peer in through the kitchen window to see if Boris was a police dog or an officer, but she couldn't be sure.

As a sun room, the poorly-named conservatory was rubbish. It faced north, and was cool and shady. As a studio, however, it was ideal, and it was the perfect place to stand when in the grip of a heatwave.

Reg's facial expression quivered and his lip curled when he saw some of the paintings that Alec had been working on.

"What do you think to his work?" Penny couldn't resist asking.

"Each to their own," he said stiffly. "He's not here now to explain his work."

She felt chastened by his reluctance to speak ill of the dead. "Of course. Yes."

He flapped the sheaf of paper at Cath. "Now, young lady. You are sure to laugh but I have discovered something new that I can do on a computer and I'm very proud of it!"

"What is this?" Cath asked. Although Reg was waving the papers at her, when Cath reached out to take them, he seemed reluctant to let go. Instead he fanned them out.

"Did you know that every website you've looked it gets stored in a list on your computer?" he said.

"Yes," Cath said. "Although we in the police often find that our dozier criminals don't know it."

"You'll be telling me you can see what people are doing in their own homes, right from the police station, next!"

Cath and Penny exchanged a look, and Penny smiled. "If you have nothing to hide…"

Reg thinned his lips. "An Englishman's home is his castle! Now look. That Alec chap, Mr Goodwin, God rest his soul, came to see me last week because he wanted to find out about two people that he used to know. I told Miss May here all about that. Carl and Amanda Fredericks, their names were. I helped him out, and left him alone with the laptop to do his searching."

"Oh! So this is his browsing history," Cath said, her eyes lighting up. "That is wonderful. Please, may we see?" She was finally able to prise it from his grasp.

Penny elbowed her way close up to Cath's side, and

peered at the sheets of paper. Reg had mastered taking a screen shot, but not yet worked out how to crop it down to the relevant part of the screen, so there was an awful lot of unnecessary stuff including a half-covered game of solitaire in progress.

"Oh …" Penny said at the same time as Cath said, "Ahh."

"I've got internet on my phone," Cath said. "Let's look this up."

Alec had been searching for combinations of Carl Fredericks and Amanda Fredericks, and "court case" and "Lincoln Crown Court" and "robbery."

"He was a court artist, wasn't he?" Penny said, as she took the paper from Cath. Cath fished around for her mobile.

"He was. So this is very interesting."

"I remembered that he did say they were friends," Reg offered. "It's funny how memory works when you get older. I am not making excuses, you know. It is just how it is. I can tell you all about my primary school but not a lot about last Tuesday. Anyway. So Alec Goodwin said that Carl and Amanda were old friends of his, you see. It came to me on the way over."

"I wonder why he suddenly wanted to get in touch with them now?" Penny mused as Cath tapped away on her phone. "What had changed in his life?"

"There isn't a lot of information on the sites he looked at," Cath said, squinting, her fingers pinching and darting to enlarge the data on the screen. "It was too long ago. I think this calls for a trip to the microfiche at the library. We're going to have to go old-school."

"I did print out one thing that was interesting," Reg said. "It's at the bottom. The court case wasn't anything to do with Carl Fredericks, you see."

"Then who?" Penny flicked through as Cath tucked her phone away.

"That's Francine," Cath said immediately.

Penny stared, her belly feeling cold. The photograph was faded and grainy, and printed out badly to boot. It seemed to have been scanned into the website that looked at notorious crimes that had happened in the East Midlands.

Even so, after the multiple layers of change and process, the woman in the photograph had a familiar air. Her hair was short and dark, and her nose was long and narrow, and her eyes were slitted.

"Francine…" Penny breathed.

Then she looked closer and deciphered the smudgy caption. "No. This was twenty years ago, and this is Amanda Fredericks on the day she was sentenced to ten years in prison."

CHAPTER NINE

Penny was halfway back to her cottage when Drew rang, offering her a meal at the rather posh gastro-pub that lay on the southern edge of town. It had a large car park, menus with curly gold writing, and something called "ambience" which meant they could charge more for their chips.

She agreed. He told her that he'd collect her at seven, and that he already had a table booked. She laughed at his presumption, but he dismissed it.

"If not you," he said, "I would have found someone else to take."

"Charming."

"Pragmatic. Anyway. I'm glad it's you and not my neighbour Terry. He talks about stamps a lot. See you later. Also, I have news…"

He rang off before she could ask him to expand on that, and she could hear the laughter in his voice.

Francine was delighted to hear that Penny had a date, and insisted on helping her to decide what to wear. Even Kali got over-excited and bounced around as Francine spread all of Penny's make-up out on the bed, and began to peer critically at the bottles and plastic containers.

"But this is all the sort of boring, corporate stuff you were wearing when you were working in television," Francine said. "Why did you keep buying it?"

"I didn't. It is *literally* the same stuff. I've never bought any more."

"Everything is so beige," Francine complained. "It doesn't really match your new funky hair or your motorbike or your attitude or anything."

"You're right." Penny stared at it all glumly. "And it's getting old now, too, so it's probably crawling with germs. I never thought about mascara having a best-before date till I saw this photo on Facebook which made me gip."

"Hang on." Francine disappeared, and returned with a large bag of her own stuff. "This is like being a teenage girl again!" She even attempted to sit cross-legged on the bed, but soon gave that up as too painful for middle-aged hips to enjoy.

As Francine messed around with eyeshadow and lip liner and myriad other pots and potions of the feminine arts, she asked about the progress with Alec Goodwin.

"It looks like murder," Penny told her, and Francine whooped, but caught herself with a horrified look.

"Oh my gosh, I am so sorry. That was terrible of me."

Penny smiled. "I understand."

"Ugh." Francine composed herself. "So who are the suspects? That's the important thing. The killer has to be found!"

"Yes, you're right. Well, Steve – you know, Ginni's nephew – he is one."

"You don't look convinced," Francine said.

"I'm not, and neither are the police. He had a motive, and he was there, and he found the body. I just don't think his motive is strong enough. Who on earth would kill over the chance to make some sculptures?"

"It wasn't that, though," Francine pointed out. "It's money, isn't it? A job. A first commission. Spring-boarding his career. People will sink to a lot, to get started in the corporate world. Don't you look back and shudder at what you put up with? Ooh, perhaps he was in on it with his aunt."

Penny remembered Agatha's assessment of Ginni. "Perhaps he was. And I can imagine Ginni killing someone if she thought she had the right reason. I can't, however, imagine her killing for *this* reason. She's an old-school battle-axe. She'd go up against a gang of club-wielding thugs to defend the weak and innocent. But this? No. But what do I know? People have layers, don't they?"

"They do," Francine said, and turned away to fiddle in the bag, looking for something. She didn't find whatever it was.

"There might be some more people on the list of suspects. Carl and Amanda Fredericks," Penny said, and explained what Reg Bailey had told them that day. Francine listened avidly.

"Have you spoken to them?"

"Cath's on the case. I did look up the Carl guy, but there wasn't a lot about him online. He is the same age as Alec, so perhaps Reg was right when he said they were friends that lost touch."

"And they must be linked through the court work!"

"Yes, but don't forget, Carl's wife went to prison…"

Francine's eyes widened. "There are so many possibilities! Are they still married, Carl and Amanda?"

"I don't know. Yet. Is that glitter you're waving at me?"

"You need a little extra sparkle!"

"I do *not*."

* * * *

The sparkle turned out to be inevitable. Francine was insistent. Drew stared at her when she opened the door to his knock.

"You … you … er, you've had your hair done," he said. "You look different. I mean nice. You look *nice*."

"Sparkly, you mean."

"What?"

"It's okay. Thank you. I'm ready to go."

Drew grinned. "Great."

He had parked at the far end of the street, where it was easier to turn the car around, and she followed him. He was a tall, broad man, and had thick wrists poking out from his turned-back shirt sleeves. Until recently, he'd been a blacksmith, although he'd favoured ornamental ironwork over shoeing horses and the like. Now, though, he was running field-craft and bush-craft courses. A local hotel had expanded into a conference centre. Apparently, what under-stimulated office workers really needed, was to learn how to cook a mushroom in a fire pit.

He didn't ask her about the case with Alec. Instead, they chatted about inconsequential things as they drove to the pub, and then they were caught up in trying to decipher the menu. The chef had had an attack of French, it seemed.

"What's a courgette flower beignet?" Drew asked.

"Deep fried in batter."

"So can you order a chocolate bar beignet in Scottish chip shops?"

"Almost certainly. Gosh, this menu is pretentious." Penny grinned. "I was in Latvia once, and they had tried to translate some of the menu items. I was so very tempted to order 'Naked Fleeing Swedish Mercenaries' but I bottled out and went for chicken breast in the end."

Drew put his menu down. "I've never even been to France."

"Haven't you?" It felt as though a gulf appeared between them. Penny had travelled the world in the course of her career. Drew had been born and raised in this handful of square miles of eastern England.

"I did go on a package trip to Spain with the lads once, though."

"Was it fun?"

"It was … messy. Quite literally. It was before camera-phones, though. So that's a relief."

"Ahh."

They ordered, and started on the wine while they waited for the main course to arrive. Both had skipped starters, on the mutual understanding that this allowed more space for pudding.

"Is this nestling, do you think?" Drew said when his steak arrived. "The menu said it would be nestling in the micro greens."

Penny peered at the blood-red meat. "That looks fairly nestley. Speaking of nettles, which we're not, sort of … how is work? Are the foraging courses going well?"

"Oh yes, and I'm really looking forward to autumn because that's when the really interesting plants grow. I've got some great fungi courses lined up. I suppose it's because I'm such a fun guy."

She groaned and stabbed into her lamb. "Your clients don't come for the jokes, do they?"

"No. To be fair, they don't. Anyway, I promised you news. I'm surprised you haven't been at my throat dragging it out of me already."

"Ha." She dangled her fork nonchalantly. "I wouldn't flatter yourself that you are *that* interesting."

"Ouch."

She smiled and leaned forward. "But come on, come on, come on. I am dying to know."

"It's about Barry Neville."

"Oh." She sat back. For some reason, she thought he was going to tell her about Alec Goodwin. "Barry, the guy that rents a – well, it's a shack – on Alec's land?"

"The same. Is he being considered a suspect in the case?"

"No. He doesn't have any motive, as far as anyone knows."

"Really?" Drew said in surprise. "Barry and Alec didn't get on, you know. In fact, I heard they hated one another."

"But Barry lived next to him."

Drew shrugged. "Maybe that's why he hated him. I don't know. Anyway, because I thought he'd be an obvious suspect, I did some digging on him. You know I've been doing some sessions down at The Acorns, right?"

"Yeah, that school for naughty kids, is that what it is?"

"I'm learning a lot about so-called naughty kids," Drew said, suddenly quite serious. "These kids aren't just acting up. They have issues. I mean, in many cases, it goes back to how they were brought up, their home lives, even medical problems, all sorts of things. It's really quite sad. They have such low self-esteem, some of them. There's one lad, just a scrap of a thing, looks twelve but he's fifteen. All he's ever been told is that he's worthless, you know? At home and at school. He's not, but now he doesn't believe it if anyone praises him. He was on my navigation session last week, and he did really well. I told him so. And then he smashed up my compass."

"He did what? The little…"

"No, no, you see, it wasn't out of spite. The teachers explained it to me. He couldn't match it up in his head, see. The worthless thing he *knows* he is, against the clever young man that I told him he was. He's started to trust me and believe me, but if he does trust and believe what I say, it means the other stuff he thinks about himself is a lie. Do you see?"

Penny sipped at her wine as she thought about it. "I am not sure, but I'm interested. Poor kid, though."

"Exactly. Being a teenager is hard enough without your own family and your own head messing you up from the inside. And this brings me to Barry Neville."

"He's not a kid."

"Nope. But when he was, he was a pupil at The Acorns."

"When? And why?"

"He's only in his early thirties. He was a pupil there fifteen years ago or so, and some of the staff remember him. There are such small classes that the teachers get to know the kids very well. Apparently he had really bad literacy issues. They'd call it dyslexia now, of course. Although some of the teachers reckoned that kids don't get enough help even these days. I tell you what, Penny, some of those teachers can't half rant when they get a cup of coffee and a head of steam up."

"I'll bet. What does it mean for the murder of Alec

Goodwin though? I would hate to suggest that someone with literacy problems was more likely to be a murderer. That's offensive. He still doesn't have a proper motive, does he?"

Drew deflated. "No, he doesn't. I don't know. Barry needs looking into, though. I would be asking why he lived there when he didn't get on with Alec, and what he saw when Alec died, and also … why he hangs around with that Steve, too."

"Oh yes. I'd forgotten about that. They had been drinking together the previous night, hadn't they? And Steve claimed to have left his phone there."

Drew nodded. "You see? There's something going on."

"Time was when you tried to put me off from looking into these things," Penny said and laughed as she pointed her fork at him. "Now look at you. You're as keen as I am."

He smiled, but ducked his head sideways and looked down. "Yes. And no. I am still concerned for you. Last time you went dashing off, following people, and ended up in all sorts of bother. I would rather that didn't happen again."

"I promise I won't randomly follow people. Or meet strange men in dark fields. Or get death threats."

"Good. So, cheesecake?"

"Sounds good. And, thanks, Drew."

"For the insight and information?"

"No, for paying. You were going to, weren't you…?

CHAPTER TEN

Penny slept in late on Saturday morning, and when she woke up, she felt groggy and disorientated.

She never usually slept in late. Not since taking on a dog, at any rate. But when she turned her head, the familiar big brown eyes were not there.

She sat up and listened intently.

Nothing.

She had had quite a bit to drink the previous night, that was true. Her head was feeling thick and woolly. She didn't drink as regularly as she had done in London, so her tolerance levels had slipped, too.

She swung her robe around her shoulders and padded down to the kitchen, expecting to see Francine sitting at the table with a coffee, entertaining Kali, but the room was empty. There was a note on the table, from Francine.

"I've gone shopping. Surprise! I walked Kali. Hope you had a good night. X."

Surprise? That boded ill. Penny put the note down and peeped around the door into the front room. There was a small, furry black shape on the sofa. It was amazing how the dog could curl into the tiniest of balls, but when you wanted to sit on the sofa too, she would somehow expand and stretch out and take up three seats to herself.

"Morning, Kali."

The dog's eyes opened slightly and her tail gave one thump. Then she went back to sleep.

"Oh, lovely to see you, too," Penny muttered with a hint of bitterness.

The unexpectedly free morning was an ideal chance for Penny to get on with her craft work. But she couldn't get into it. She hated the idea of being a temperamental artist who could only work when the inspiration was right – *plumbers didn't wait for the bathroom muse before they picked up a wrench, so artists shouldn't wait for the painting muse*, she thought. And yet she stared at a sheet of doodles for half an hour, and got nowhere.

It was almost a relief when the front door slammed

and Francine shouted "hellooooo" from the hallway. When Penny got to the door, she saw that Kali was on her feet, tail wagging, greeting Francine with exuberance.

Disloyal dog.

Francine was wearing a hat so wide it knocked against walls. She hung it up on a hook and kicked off her sandals, coming down to the kitchen in her bare feet. "It's going to rain," she said. "The sky is almost black."

"Ahh," Penny said. "I can blame my headache on the changing weather, then. And not the vast amount of alcohol I drank last night."

Francine looked sceptical but she didn't correct her. *She never did*, Penny realised.

Maybe that was why she listened to loony theories about everything. She was so open and honest that she didn't like to criticise anyone or anything.

As a test, she said, "You know that some people think that everything in the world is controlled by eight-foot-tall lizard men?"

"Really?" Francine said. "We'd notice that, surely. Where do they live?"

My point is proved, Penny thought. *Most people's first*

reaction would be to say "what nonsense" but Francine is too nice. It was kind of sweet, though.

"I don't know," she said in reply to Francine. "I think it sounds barmy. Don't you?"

"It does sound rather unlikely. I wonder what made them think of it in the first place, though? They must have had some ... well, not quite evidence, but some reason. Anyway. Lizards, ugh. I've bought you something! I can't wait to show you."

They went back into the kitchen and Francine emptied out her carrier bag onto the work counter, as the table was now covered in sketches and pencils.

"Look!" Francine said dramatically.

Penny looked. "Oh. Oh, you really shouldn't have..."

"There's eyeshadow and some wonderful matte foundation and I thought this glittery eye liner was really you. What do you think?"

Penny suppressed her sigh. "I don't really go out often enough to justify all this... but, thank you. How much do I owe you?"

Now it was Francine's turn to sigh. "Nothing. It's a gift, from me to you!"

"You really don't need to. I appreciate all the things you're doing for me, but..."

"It's nothing! I owe you, I really do. I must not be a burden here. Come on. It's fine." Francine gathered it all back into the bag and left it on the counter. "Now, let's get the kettle on and I'll tell you what I saw in the market this morning."

"And what was that?" Penny asked, trying to sound interested. She assumed Francine had spotted a particularly clever kitchen item on Mop Woman's stall, or a new range of nylon overalls.

"You told me about Ginni the florist's nephew, Steve, right?"

"Yes." Penny perked up instantly.

"I think I saw him. He's tall but a bit gangly, with lank hair, right?"

"Yes, but that's most of the lads around here, isn't it?"

"Not really. He's the only one with hair hanging down like it does. Haven't you noticed the fashion is for short hair with longer on top, and symbols razored into the back? Even out here, the kids want to be trendy."

Now Francine pointed it out, Penny had to concede it

was true. "My powers of observation definitely need some work."

"Well, I did some observing for you. This lad, Steve, he was arguing with a stallholder in the market, you see."

"What about?" Penny asked.

"He was just buying a second hand dvd. Then he started going on to the man at the stall that he had been overcharged. It was stupid really, because the prices are all on the stickers, so he knew how much it was going to cost. He handed the money over and then acted all surprised when he didn't get change. I've seen people do it before, and it makes them look foolish. He started saying how he could get it for cheaper and brand new somewhere else."

"What did the stallholder say?"

"He told him he was welcome to go somewhere else, then."

"Did he get his money back?"

"No, he shouted a bit and then walked off. I saw him afterwards, sitting on a wall, smoking a cigarette. His hands were shaking." Francine beamed at her observational prowess. "I noticed that specially."

"Hmm."

"Hmm? Don't you think this makes him more of a suspect?"

"What, because he is a consumer activist on a crusade against overcharging?" Penny shook her head.

"No, because it shows he's angry and impulsive."

"We all have days like that," Penny said. "But I'll make a note. Thank you."

Francine looked crestfallen. Penny picked up the bag of unwanted make up. "I'm going to go and try that eyeliner," she said, and was rewarded with a smile.

* * * *

Penny sat in her bedroom and stared at herself in the mirror. The eyeliner was pretty good. It made her feel sad.

Because it was time to have that talk with Francine.

She found her in the back garden. The grey, leaden sky was oppressive but the rain had not yet started. Francine was dead-heading some of the flowers in the borders, and Kali was sniffing the lawn, looking for the very best – or, indeed worst – place to dig a hole for fun.

"Francine. We need to talk."

Francine looked up and she seemed startled, wary and almost scared. "What about?" She didn't come forward. She remained by the flower bed, the secateurs hanging loosely in her hand.

"We need to talk about you staying here," Penny said. "This is difficult because I don't want you to feel unwanted. It's not that I don't want you here, but..." She tailed off, hoping that Francine could fill in the blanks. *Don't make me say it*, she pleaded. *Don't make me actually ask you to leave. Gosh, I am such a coward.*

Francine folded. She crumpled slowly so that she was kneeling on the lawn, and she rested her hands in her lap. "I've tried to be nice," she whispered.

"No one could be nicer than you."

"That's what *he* said."

"Who?"

"Darrell. Well, he didn't say it to my face. It's what I overheard. He said other stuff, too. They all did. All the production company."

"About you?"

"Yes, about me. About how wet and silly I was. How easy I was to fool just because I want to see the best in

138

people. But I'm not fooled, Penny, and I never was. I *choose* to think good things. I wanted to think good things about Darrell, but he was laughing with them about how he'd ..."

"What?" Penny exploded in righteous anger. She was kneeling on the ground, at Francine's side, instantly. Kali leaped over as well, keen to not be left out. "What did he do? Where is he? I'll..."

"No, no. He just took me for a ride. He took advantage of my good nature. I paid for stuff, more stuff than I should have. I agreed to go on dates out of my comfort zone. I just wanted to please him. And all the while it was like a bet with his mates to see what I'd say yes to."

"He didn't..." Penny left the question hanging, but Francine knew what she meant.

"No. He never forced ..."

"I'm still angry."

"I know. I feel silly. I am silly. It wasn't the reason I came here. It was *part* of the reason. It was all building up together. And it made me realise how alone I was in a place and a company where everyone thought the worst of everyone else and therefore acted accordingly."

"Have you resigned, or taken a sabbatical?"

"Resigned. I rented out my flat, too."

"Oh goodness. On a six month lease?"

"Yes." Francine looked up, and her eyes were watery. "Don't worry. I don't expect to live with you for six months. And you're right. I need to move out. I suppose I hoped I'd have some kind of epiphany, like you did, and it would all fall into place. I'm forty-two and it was all supposed to be sorted by now. You know, life."

"I'm older than you and it hasn't fallen into place for me yet," Penny said. "Growing up into an adult is a myth."

"But I want to grow up," Francine said, sounding plaintive. "I've always had men after me, but none of them lasted and I don't know why. I've worked hard and tried to please but it has never been enough. So I made a drastic change, like you did, but I still feel adrift. What now?"

Penny thought about some of the men that had dated Francine. They had never been very social together in London, but the world of television was small and so she knew of some of the relationships. To a man, they had been attracted to Francine's little-girl demeanour and had soon revealed themselves to be overly dominant, overly needy or simply overbearing.

"Stop trying to please," Penny said. "Be yourself."

"I am myself," Francine said. "That is who I am. I want to please others."

It was true. No one was more herself than Francine. "Maybe …" Penny said, thinking slowly and carefully, "Maybe you're just fine as you are, but London wasn't ever the right place for you, and it's going to take time for you to settle down. Look. Don't worry about finding somewhere else to live. Stay here a little while longer." It was hard to say, but it was the right thing to say. She was ashamed to find she'd never really considered Francine to have deeper feelings before.

"Thank you. Do you mean it?"

That hurt. "I am *always* going to be honest with you. I promise."

"Thank you again. I really liked Darrell, too, you know. I really liked him. I thought he was the one. I thought I was not working hard enough at the relationship. I thought he was being very kind and generous in giving me chance after chance."

"That sounds really unhealthy."

"I think so, now, when I look back. But why was he

like that? Why would anyone be so mean?"

"People can be horrible."

"Why?"

She thought about Drew and what he'd said about the pupils at the school. "Perhaps they had issues in their past and they can't function properly," she said, and she saw immediately that she had finally said the right thing.

It was easier for Francine to feel sympathy than anger. "Yes, of course. Poor Darrell."

I'd punch Darrell in the face if I saw him, Francine thought. "Poor Darrell," she murmured. *And then I would spit in his fancy London coffee.*

Thinking of coffee made her think of Alec Goodwin, and it seemed a good change of subject.

"I know I'm not all sweetness and light," Penny said. "Not like you. But I admire that in you and I don't think you should lose it. Don't fret too much about people being mean. It's their problem, not yours. Stay nice and you'll always have friends – true friends. What's the alternative? Darrell will probably end up like Alec Goodwin, living alone and reclusive."

"Maybe he was happy living like that," Francine

countered. She, too, seemed grateful for the conversational segue. "I wouldn't want to judge another's lifestyle choice."

"Perhaps. I wonder why Alec was like that, though? I wonder what happened? I mean, he used to have friends. Carl Fredericks, for one."

"Yes ... have you found out anything more about him?"

Penny shook her head. "Cath's doing the official digging."

"Why wait for her?"

"Because she's the police."

"Ahh, details," Francine said, and laughed. She wiped away a stray tear, and then patted Penny's knee. "Why don't you go out and look at his bulb business. It's not far away, is it?"

"What would I learn from that?"

"You learn a lot from seeing where people live, and how. I did ..."

"When? What are you talking about?"

Francine bit her lip but she smiled slightly. "Well, I went to see this famous, reclusive artist myself, you know."

"When?"

"Oh, ages ago now. Well, last Thursday."

"The Thursday before the weekend that he died?"

"Yes."

"Oh my goodness. What was he like? Did he show any signs of stress or strain? What did he say?"

"Don't get excited," Francine said. "Nothing. None of that. I didn't see him at all. It was evening. I walked down and I was just going to look at his house from the outside. But when I got there, I thought, well, I might as well go and knock on the door. Maybe he'd show me his paintings."

"Oh my…"

"He didn't answer. So I went around the side of the house. I wasn't snooping, I promise. I saw there was a conservatory or something along the back, and I peeped through a window. I could see his easels and clay work and everything, and I was sure I saw him disappear through a door, so I knocked on the glass, but he didn't come out. And then some dogs started barking behind me and I was afraid, so I left pretty quickly. And that's all."

"Why didn't you tell me this before?" Penny asked.

"It wasn't relevant. Okay, I felt a bit like I shouldn't have gone there. And then I wondered if he was already dead when I went around, and I was sort of afraid I'd be a suspect."

"Oh, Francine. Anyway, Reg Bailey saw him on Friday, don't forget."

"Thank goodness!"

Penny laughed. "You ninny. No, you're not a suspect."

"The thing is, though," Francine said. "Those dogs of his. They were barking like mad and one of them started to run towards me over the garden. So if he was really killed, the dogs would have been barking, wouldn't they? So that would have alerted Barry Neville, who lives next door."

"I think they are Barry's dogs, too."

"They were in Alec's garden," Francine pointed out.

Barry Neville was coming up too often in conversation and Penny's suspicions were growing. "Interesting," she said. "And maybe you're right. I think a trip out to see Carl Fredericks in on the cards. *And* Barry Neville."

"I knew it," Francine said.

CHAPTER ELEVEN

"Hi Drew. How are you?" Penny said on the phone on Sunday morning.

"I'm doing okay. How's your hangover?"

"How did you know I had a hangover?"

"Intuition. Also, you drank a bottle of wine on Friday night and you sang a song about fairies and elves."

"Oh, yeah, that. It was a lovely meal, by the way. Thank you."

"You're welcome. But that's not why you're calling me, is it? Out with it, Penny."

"Okay. Well, you know how I said I wouldn't go off following people any more?"

Drew sighed. "Yes."

"So, I want to go and look at where Carl Fredericks lives. And I'm doing this the sensible way – by asking you if you would like to come?"

"Hang on," Drew said. "The sensible way is by dragging me into it as well?"

"Yes. And you did say, ages ago, that you'd take me out on the Fens and tell me about them."

"I seem to remember you poo-pooing the idea, though. You said you couldn't imagine anything worse than a guided tour of a sluice."

"A woman may change her mind," Penny said with exaggerated aloofness. "Are you free today?"

"From midday, I am. Okay then. I'll pick you up, shall I?"

* * * *

"Flat" seemed like the understatement of the year. The Fens weren't landscape. It was the total absence of landscape that disorientated and confused Penny as she stared out of the window. The oppressive weather had broken overnight, and the day was bright and clear and fresher than it had previously been. Still, they had the windows rolled down and their elbows out, and she wore large sunglasses to feel a bit like Jackie O.

"There's nothing here," she said. "Nothing. Just sky."

"Sky isn't nothing," Drew said. "There's clouds. Birds. Colours."

"Yes but other than that, there's nothing, and it goes on forever. It's actually like being at sea."

"It was sea, once, and I think one day it will be sea again, and cabbages will cost more."

Penny laughed. "Excuse me?"

"This is all artificial," Drew explained. "As far as I understand it, it was marshland for centuries. Aeons, however long one of them is. I think the Romans did some drainage and cut some ditches, but when they left, it was pretty much a lawless place. Until, of course, Charles the First needed to raise some cash because Parliament was getting all bolshie with him."

"He did ask for it," Penny said. "The bolshiness, I mean."

"He was misunderstood. Anyway, so he started to sell off parcels of this marshland to rich folks, telling them they could drain it and use it as agricultural land and they'd be rich. The Dutch had done it, and they had developed some techniques for draining the soil."

"Yeah, but where does the water go?" she asked.

"It's still there. That's why there are so many pumping stations and sluices out here. It's continual. Much of this land is actually below sea level."

"That must be at a high risk of flooding, then. Why bother? This area isn't that big."

Drew laughed. "Look at it."

"What am I looking at?"

"Crops. Fields. Incredibly fertile land. I mean, a seriously large proportion of much of our market garden produce comes from here. That's what I mean by the price of cabbages going up if it all floods again. This peaty soil is perfect. And not just for cabbages, either." Drew slowed the car down. There were no vehicles to be seen, either behind them or in front of them. The road was arrow-straight, with a ditch either side. "Look in there."

"What is it?"

"I'm guessing it was tulips. I should bring you back in springtime when it's just ablaze with colour from horizon to horizon. Honestly, now people come from Holland to see *our* bulb fields."

"And that's what Carl Fredericks does," Penny said. "Grows flowers."

"Bulbs, I think," Drew said.

They drove on. The road occasionally made inexplicable right-angled turns, and they passed sporadic outcrops of houses and buildings that looked tiny, dwarfed by the empty sky.

Eventually they came to a junction. To the right, the road ran on in a straight line, heading for Boston. There was a sign pointing to the left, advertising Fredericks' Bulb Growers. The road was tarmac, but single-track with grass, very neatly clipped, close to both sides.

Drew pulled into the turning but then stopped and killed the engine. "Come on," he said. "Get out for a moment."

Penny unfolded herself and stretched her legs as she stood up straight. She wrinkled her nose. "What's that smell? I mean, it's not unpleasant."

"Just pollen and agriculture and stuff," he said. "The one smell you don't want to encounter out here is when they're dredging the dykes."

"I *beg* your pardon?" Penny said. "I have got to assume

that has a totally different meaning to what it would sound like in London…"

Drew raised his eyebrows innocently. "The dykes? The narrow drainage channels that run along the edge of the fields. In some places, dyke means a raised bank, but not here. The Romans dug the Carr Dyke, as it happens, and it still exists. But they get clogged with weeds and so on, so periodically they need to drag all the vegetable matter from the bottom, and they just dump it on the banks. And it stinks."

"Delightful." Penny gazed around, staring out to the shimmering horizon. The atmosphere was hazy with heat and the colours were washed out and faded. "What am I supposed to be looking at?"

"The little things," Drew said. "Here." He waved his hand and pointed at the grassy verge. "Marsh mallow."

She blinked in surprise at the purple-flowered plant. "Is it edible?"

"The roots are, and that's where marshmallows came from, originally. And here, orchids!"

"Oh my goodness." Penny bent to look at the delicate drooping blooms. "It's a proper chequer-board pattern on the petals. I have never seen anything like it."

"Come up here." He led her up a bank that divided the road from a dyke. "Aha! I had hoped to spot kingfishers, but there is something almost as good. In those rushes, there. Do you see it?"

Penny peered until the grey statue made sense to her vision. "Oh, a heron!"

"A hernshaw. Yes, a heron. I always think they look like little wizards, cloaked and waiting…"

"You poet, you."

"There he goes."

They waited until the great bird had slowly flapped away. A few hundred yards along, there were two swans bobbing idly in the water. A green flash shot past, and she jumped.

"Dragonfly," Drew said. "There."

Once she knew what to look for, the air was alive with things. Now she knew why Drew had stopped. All the Fens' empty nothing was positively teeming with life, but you couldn't see it from a car window.

"Well, let's get on," Drew said at last. "Ready to meet Carl Fredericks?"

"Yes. I hope he's in."

* * * *

He was in.

They drove into a large, neat courtyard, bounded on three and a half sides by large sheds with brick walls and corrugated iron roofs. One of the sheds had its roller shutter open, and a small white van was backed up to it. There was a man with thinning brown hair loading plastic trays into the back of it, and he looked up as he heard their vehicle approach.

Penny wiped her palms on her trousers, and Drew caught the nervous movement. "Are you okay?" he asked. "I thought you were used to all this."

"It's always gone wrong before," she pointed out.

The man was walking towards them now, so they got out of the car. Drew stayed back, leaning against the bonnet, and Penny forced herself forward. She channelled all her confidence, remembering that she had once arm-wrestled a Russian oligarch in a nightclub in St Petersburg.

She had lost, but she'd won some respect.

Hopefully, this wouldn't come to arm-wrestling, she thought. She thrust out her hand. "Hi! I'm Penny May."

"Now then," he said, his Lincolnshire accent adding in a few extra vowels. "What can I do for you?"

"Are you Carl Fredericks?"

"Ar. I am."

She bit back her smile at his piratical assertion. "I'm pleased to meet you. I understand you knew Alec Goodwin?"

"Ar." Carl folded his arms but he kept his smile on his face. *That was odd. It should have faded by now.* "Can I ask what capacity you're acting in?"

It was a tricky question to answer. She was only unofficially linked to the police, after all, and they would deny all knowledge if she got herself into bother. She hated to lie, but it didn't harm to fudge the truth a little. She said, brightly, "I'm involved in Upper Glenfield's arts and crafts scene and Alec was working with us on the Sculpture Trail."

Carl's facial expression was tight and fixed. He seemed to realise this, and rubbed at his cheeks. Finally his smile faded. "And what has the Sculpture Trail to do with me?" he said. "I'm sorry if that sounds rude. But…"

He tailed off. Penny decided to capitalise on his

uncertainty, and just go for the steamroller option. She said, "Of course, of course, and I appreciate you taking the time to talk with us." *You have no choice*, she thought. *I shall simply act as if you've already agreed.* "As you and Alec were old friends, we hoped you could offer some insight into his art and work and character." A blast of inspiration hit out of nowhere. "We – the residents of Upper Glenfield – are so grateful to the work he did in our community and the recognition he brought that we intend to create a fitting memorial to the man, and we were hoping you might offer some background to his life before he came to Glenfield." She didn't dare look around at Drew. His mouth would be hanging open. He'd never seen her in full flow; her verbal flights of fancy had got her out of trouble in every continent in the world.

"And you're asking *me*," he said, somewhat flatly. There was no hint of a smile now.

"Yes. You were friends, weren't you…?"

"Ar. Yes. Yes!" Carl forced a new and fake grin onto his face, and brushed his hands together as if he'd been doing something messy. "We were. But, you see, I don't think I can help you. I had heard of his death. It do sound tragic and I don't wish ill on no one, but we weren't friends much lately, really, you know, you see?"

In amongst the flim-flam, Penny hunted for real information. "Had you lost touch?"

He nodded furiously. "We had, we had. Ar. Yes, we had."

"What a shame. He used to be a court artist, didn't he?"

"Ar. He did."

"And have you always worked in the bulb business?"

"Oh, I started up about twenty-five years ago. Bit unusual really, not being born into it. I knew I wanted to be in business, and this came along, as an opportunity, like. So I took it."

"I admire that," Penny said. "That solid sense of entrepreneurship. Well done. And so you and Alec lost touch and he never got to see all your success, then? Or did he? When was the last time that you did meet?"

He had been relaxing but her move into more questioning caught him off guard. "I, er, well. You know, it is funny you should ask, really. He rang me up, he did, not so long back. Um, Friday gone, it was."

"Oh! He just got in touch, out of the blue?"

He was nodding, then shaking his head, then nodding again. "Yes, ar, yes. But not to speak to me, though, no. He was after Mandy, really."

"Mandy?" Penny said. The name nagged at her. She'd heard of a Mandy recently. *Where, who?*

Carl turned away. "It's all in the past. Mandy, my ex-wife. You'll understand if I don't want to talk about it. I'm sorry I can't be of any help. I don't think I'm the man you're looking for, but good luck and all that, with the memorial. To be honest, I'm pretty surprised about that. I didn't reckon he were a community sort of man, living like he did."

Mandy. *Amanda*. Penny couldn't let it lie, not now. "Oh, he was still something of a local celebrity. Quite well-known, really. Your ex-wife, Mandy ... does she live around here?"

"That's what he wanted to know. Nah, she's in Lincoln."

"So you're still in touch with her? That's so good, you know, when divorces can be amicable..."

The look that Carl shot her was not one of amity. "We

ain't in touch. Nah."

"Do you have her address or anything? Perhaps she can help us with Alec and the memorial."

That made Carl laugh in a dry and unsettling way. "I doubt it. Ar, doubt it." He swore and wrinkled his nose. "Nah, I don't have her details. Look her up yourself."

"Mandy Fredericks…" Penny said, angling.

He responded almost automatically. "Jones. She went back to Jones."

And that was why they couldn't find Amanda Fredericks listed anyway. She wanted to punch the air. "Thank you so much. You've been very helpful."

He shrugged. "Nah, I ain't, but that's how it goes. Good luck with the memorial thing. I suppose he probably was the most exciting thing to have happened in Upper Glenfield."

"Do you know it?"

He shook his head. "I been through it. Just another nothing town in the middle of nowhere. Take care, now."

He waved and half-turned, and she knew it was time to go before she overstepped the mark and increased his suspicion. Drew slipped into the driver's seat and she was just opening the passenger door when Carl surprised her by speaking again.

"Seeing as you live there, and that, you might have heard whether his death was accidental or not. Do you know?"

It had been in the regional papers, but maybe he didn't read them. "They aren't one hundred per cent sure but they are currently treating it as suspicious."

"Suspicious? What, like murder?"

She nodded, and watched his face carefully. He looked genuinely shocked. "Yes, like murder," she said. And, because it had been in the paper too, she added, "Poisoned."

He actually gasped, and swore again. "No way. What with?"

"They don't know yet. But they will find out, I'm sure."

"Ar, no doubt, no doubt. So who could have done it, though? Murder's got to have suspects, ain't it?"

"Well," she said, deciding on an impetuous risk, "He spoke to you on Friday, didn't he?"

"Nah, nah, it ain't me you should be thinking of there. Remember he wanted to speak to *her*. So you wanna be looking there. Had he annoyed anyone in the town, though?"

She couldn't now say that he had kept himself to himself, after having claimed he was an active pillar of the community. So she said, "Hmm, no, not really. Anyway, thank you again for your time. Good luck with your, um, bulbs."

"Right. Ar. Thanks."

She slid into the passenger seat and turned to smile broadly at Drew. "Let's go."

They didn't discuss it until they had driven about a mile. Penny let her eyes unfocus as the landscape blurred past. "He was pretty cagey, don't you think?"

"Ar," he said, and she laughed at his imitation.

"And now we know that Amanda Fredericks is Mandy Jones. That will help."

"Ar. Sorry, yes. And what about that stuff about not having had anything to do with Alec lately?"

"Well, they'd only spoken on the phone."

Drew shook his head. "I don't believe that," he said. "Because of when he said he was surprised at him being a 'community sort of man' because of 'living like he did'. How did he know how Alec lived?"

"Oh. You're right," Penny said. She let her eyes close

and replayed the whole conversation with Carl. "He knew a lot more than he was saying, didn't he?"

CHAPTER TWELVE

The driving and the knock-on effect of her late night conspired against Penny and she awoke with a start when the car engine died.

"Aroughahh," she mumbled. "Oh."

"Good evening, sleepy head," Drew said. "You were away with the fairies there."

"What time is it?"

"It's gone five. I took the long way home because you looked so peaceful there, and your snoring was hardly distracting me from the road at all."

"I don't snore."

He laughed. "It must be like sweating, then. Men perspire and women merely glow? Men snore and women simply ... loudly snuffle. Anyway. Here we are. Thank you for asking me to come along. I want to say that I was pretty impressed at how you handled him. You do have a knack. I can see why Cath asked you to get involved."

She was inordinately pleased at his praise. "Thank you, and thanks for coming with me."

"It's all right. It was an adventure. Now, get yourself inside and if I were you, I would go straight to bed."

* * * *

She didn't go to bed, of course. As soon as she let herself in, she was besieged by both Kali and Francine. Kali wanted her belly rubbing, and Francine wanted every detail about her meeting with Carl Fredericks – and her journey with Drew.

"He showed me a heron," Penny said.

"What else did you do?"

"We talked."

"What *else* did you do?"

Penny sighed with exasperation. "It's not like that."

"But you want it to be."

"Sometimes I do, and sometimes I don't. Anyway, listen. You know we couldn't find out about Amanda

Fredericks, except that she'd gone to prison twenty years ago? She's divorced now, and called Mandy Jones."

"Excellent!" Francine picked up her coat from the back of the sofa. "It's starting to come together. Right. Are you ready, or do you want to eat first?"

"Ready for what?"

"Well, you said yesterday that a trip was on the cards. Carl Fredericks, and Barry Neville. You've been to see Carl, so now let's go and see Barry."

"Now?"

"Well, like I said, we *could* eat first..."

Penny saw that Francine was too excited. She had probably been daydreaming about it all day while Penny was out.

She conceded defeat, and said, "Let me get a sweatshirt to put on. I'll be ready in a moment. Shall we walk down or do you want to drive?"

"Let's walk."

* * * *

It was a pleasant evening. Francine chattered as they

walked.

"Steve is totally changing everything that Alec had planned for the Sculpture Trail, apparently," she said. "I got talking to that woman that you know, Mary. She asked after you, by the way."

"Oh, did she? She's a gossip but I like her. She's quite lonely. So what's Steve doing, then? Is the deadline still the same?"

"Yes," Francine said. "Everything needs to be done by the first of August for the big Summer Fair. Which means they only have a few weeks, and to be honest, he can't possibly get it done by then. I mean, I admire youthful exuberance and confidence but he should have stuck with Alec's designs. Alec had a series of wooden carved posts all drawn up, and ready to be done. Although I don't know how long it takes to carve a wooden pole. Everything's been delayed."

"What's Steve planning instead?"

"Clay tiles, on top of the posts. They've bought the wooden poles already, you see."

"Clay tiles? They won't last in the weather."

Francine nodded. "I know. It all seems a bit daft to

me. Ah. The police tape is still everywhere."

"The duty copper isn't there, though. And look, the tape's on a loop, it's not attached properly." Penny picked up one end and pulled it free of the gatepost. They slipped inside and she replaced it carefully before they continued up the driveway. They avoided the dark, silent house and made for the shack at the far end.

There was a light on in the window, although it wasn't yet dark. As Penny and Francine crunched along the gravel, which petered out into a dusty path, two squat and noisy bull terriers came barging out of nowhere and thundered towards them.

Francine squealed and jumped behind Penny, who simply shouted, "Sit!" at the pair.

Both dogs skidded to a halt, and sat. Their mouths were open, tongues lolling and their hips were waggling as their tails thrashed in delighted greeting.

"You pair of puddings," Penny said, chiding them. "What are you? Puddings."

The door to the small building opened and a stocky figure emerged. He was jowly and had a number of chins, and his beer belly hung over his faded and scuffed jeans.

But his smile was wide and warm.

"Now then! Bob, Cassandra, come here."

The two dogs gave one more longing look at the visitors, and then dashed back to their master. He bent and rubbed them both behind the ears, affectionately swearing at them, before ordering them back into the house. He pulled the door to, and came towards Penny and Francine.

"Evening ladies. What can I do you for, ha ha."

"Hi. Are you Barry Neville?"

"Depends on if he's done anything wrong, ha ha. Who's asking?" He kept on smiling, and Penny couldn't see any malice in his broad face.

"I'm Penny and this is Francine."

"How do Penny, and how do Francine. Yeah okay. I'm Barry. What have I done? Nothing bad, I hope. Have I won the lottery, ha ha?"

Penny smiled at him. "Not as far as I know, sorry. Actually we were just wondered about Alec Goodwin, really."

"Were you." He said it flatly, and his smile faded right away. There were no more jokey laughs at the end of every sentence. "You and every other nosey parker in this town,

I reckon. I lived near the bloke. Didn't have to talk to him, though, did I? So I didn't."

"Isn't your house rented from him?"

"Yeah. It is."

"But you didn't get on?"

"No. We didn't." Barry put his hand out behind him and pushed his door open again. The two bull terriers had been eagerly waiting behind the door for just the chance, and bounded out again. They dashed back up to Penny and Francine, and this time Barry made no move to call them off.

"So, er, which one is Bob and who is Cassandra?" Penny said brightly. "I've got a Rottie myself."

' "Bob's the one who'll bite your face off and Cassandra's the one who will gnaw your leg off," he said. "Ha … ha."

"Are they Staffies? Staffordshire bull terriers?"

"Yeah. If you'll excuse me, ladies, I'll get back to my tea."

He slammed back into his house, all humour and smiles totally gone, and left Penny and Francine outside with the dogs. Both dogs were on their backs, presenting their round bellies to the sky, their wide faces open and laughing.

"Daft things." Penny shook her head at them. "Well, I guess that's all we're going to find out."

"Yes, let's go," said Francine hastily, already retreating along the path towards the gravelled area.

Penny waved goodbye to the dogs and followed Francine. "Wait up. You're not scared of dogs, are you? I mean, I know Kali ran at you the first time you met her, but you soon became friends."

"I don't mind Kali, now that I know her, but I'm not keen on dogs, no. And those are pit bulls, aren't they." She quickened her pace. "They eat babies."

"Oh for goodness' sake! They were Staffies, not pit bulls. Any dog can be bad or good. It depends on the owner."

"Well, and what of the owner?" Francine slowed down as they reached the road. The ducked around the tape and began walking up the lonely, deserted road in the direction of town. "He was all laughter and joking until you mentioned Alec. And then, boom! He couldn't wait to get rid of us."

"Yeah, you're right about that. Very odd."

Francine stopped suddenly. "Is this his closest neighbour?" she asked, pointing at a house set back from the road.

Penny looked back. "It looks like it." From this point, there was a scattering of detached houses before the main residential part of Upper Glenfield began.

"Right. Let's go and talk to them about Barry."

"Barry? Don't you mean Alec?"

"No," Francine said decisively, pushing open the ornate metal gate. "Barry. He seemed very strange to me."

Penny could only scamper up behind as Francine strode to the front door and knocked the brass lion's head. It wasn't long before they were greeted by a very tall, very broad-shouldered woman of indeterminate age, with ironed-straight black hair and more Goth make-up than Penny had seen in one place since the early nineties.

"Hello," the woman said, keeping the door half-closed as she peered from one to the other. "I don't buy from the doorstep. Or go in for being converted. And I already know who I vote for. So…"

"It's okay," Francine said. "We're none of the above. We're investigating the death of Alec Goodwin. I'm sure you're fascinated with it."

Penny cringed, and waved her hands in the air like she was swatting flies. "I am *so* sorry. What my friend means is … um …"

The woman raised one pencil-thin arched eyebrow. "I knew of Alec and his work but I would hardly say I'm fascinated."

"But you're a …" Francine said.

"…accountant?" the woman finished.

Penny took charged and elbowed Francine aside with no ceremony. "What about Barry?" she asked politely. "Barry Neville, that lives on Alec's land. That's who we are actually interested in."

The woman didn't open the door any further, but she graced them with a slight smile. "Oh, Barry. He's harmless, really. He's got a mouth on him. He thinks he's funny but he's not really a bad sort."

"What about his dogs?" Francine said.

"Ahh, those pair. Yes, well, they're as harmless as Barry is. Except that he needs to keep them under better control. They roam around all over the place. They've even got up here, and dug holes in my lawn. Bit of a nightmare, really, when they run out in the middle of the road. How they haven't caused a bad accident, I do not know."

Ahh, thought Penny, *the universal conversational glue of dogs and animals in general. Sometimes I'm really glad to be British. We won't talk about important stuff unless it's through the filter of the weather, our pets, or the price of fuel.* "I suppose they caused chaos for Alec, too."

"I'll bet. It was no wonder he was trying to get poor Barry evicted."

"Oh! Was he, indeed. How long had Barry lived there?"

"Four years, I think. I've been here just about the same length of time. And the gossip locally is that they haven't exchanged a civil word for three and a half years."

"Wow," Penny and Francine both said together.

The woman nodded. "Luckily it's not so easy to just evict someone without reason these days. I helped Barry out a bit with that. I told him to get down the Citizen's Advice Bureau and everything. Helped him with some forms. I can't stand to see someone being targeted."

"Well, yes," said Francine, "but if his dogs were a problem…"

"Alec's fences were the problem, really," the woman

said firmly.

There was an awkward pause. Penny said, finally, "Thank you for your time. We appreciate it."

"Are you with the police?" she asked.

"Not exactly," Penny said. "I'm a concerned citizen and I am involved in the arts scene locally ..."

"Oh, wait!" the woman said, opening the door a little wider. "Yes, you're that London woman who sorted out the Warren Martin case, aren't you!"

"I am." She couldn't keep the note of pride out of her voice.

"You're shorter than I thought you would be," the woman said. "Good luck."

The door closed. Penny turned to Francine and they nodded at one another, staying quiet until they were off the woman's property and on their way back to Upper Glenfield.

CHAPTER THIRTEEN

"Salad or cake?"

"What?"

"Salad or cake?" Cath repeated. Her voice was fuzzy and distant, like she was driving and speaking to Penny on her hands-free set in her car.

"Cake, always."

"Great. I'll meet you by the Cathedral at midday."

"Will you?" Penny said.

"Yes. Gotta go. Bye!"

Penny rolled her eyes and tucked her phone away. Kali was looking up at her with patient expectation, and they continued on the walk. It was Monday morning, and Penny had explained to Francine that while she was very grateful for all the walks she was doing with Kali, Penny felt excluded. She missed the quiet time with her dog. Francine had been reserved, hiding her distress that her good intentions had caused more upset, but Penny felt relieved that she'd finally got it off her chest.

Strangely, she was also getting used to Francine being around. It was a comfort to know that Kali wasn't going to be on her own.

I'm in danger of taking Francine's presence for granted, Penny thought to herself once she got home. She started to ease into her motorcycle gear. She wanted to give her old motorbike a spin, and now the hot weather was breaking, it was just the right temperature to chug along the quiet back lanes to Lincoln to meet Cath. Francine's reaction to the classic bike was one of mingled horror and pure envy. She thought that anything with two wheels was a death-trap, but she couldn't deny the beauty and the elegance of the M21 with its shiny chrome and its low roar.

The ride up through the ripening fields of crops was enjoyable. Although the Fenland roads were flat and straight, the landscape changed into rolling hills as it approached the ancient cathedral city of Lincoln. The roads swept around in broad curves, and the villages were older and prettier – and the houses were far less affordable.

As Penny got closer to Lincoln, the traffic got heavier. She took the back way, avoiding the main A15 road, instead skirting alongside the back of the vast airfield of RAF Waddington. The usual plane spotters were lingering the lay-bys but most of them would be at the designated viewing area on the main road south of Lincoln, staring at the huge planes with the odd cigar shapes on the top. Drew had told Penny what they were called, but she couldn't remember. It was all to do with surveillance, anyway. She craned her neck upwards, hoping to see the far more remarkable and interesting sight of the Red Arrows Display Team practising in the sky. They were based to the north of Lincoln but often treated the local residents to elaborate air shows, as they ran through their breath-taking displays.

The sky was blue and clear today. She slowed as she reached the residential areas and it took her as long to get through Lincoln's city centre traffic as it had done to get from her house to the outskirts of the city.

She found a decent car park to leave her bike, dragged a heavy chain through the wheels for added security, and slung her helmet onto her arm as she walked through the busy pedestrian streets. The Cathedral sat atop a steep hill, called Steep Hill, the locals not being known for their inventive naming. Walking up it necessitated the use of a handrail so she had parked at the top, and it was a short walk to the large square that contained the Cathedral, the castle, and a tasteful smattering of gift shops and pubs. Cath was lurking in the cool shade of the Gothic doors.

"You're on duty," Penny said, taking in Cath's neat dark suit.

"Lunch break. I've brought cake. Shall we grab some cans of pop and sit in the sun?"

"If we can wrestle a bench free from some tourists, sure."

Once they were seated and settled, Cath opened. "So. I don't know what you've been up to, but Carl Fredericks turned up at the police station first thing this morning."

"Oh, did he?" Penny attempted to sound and look innocent. She pulled the paper wrapper from the edge of the carrot cake that Cath had passed to her. "How interesting."

"Yeah, he said he'd had a visitation from some lunatic woman with red hair and a tall bloke with big arms. So I knew it was you and Drew."

"Lunatic? I was behaving pretty normally. Ask Drew! I was really *trying*."

Cath raised her eyebrows. "What did he say to you, this Carl? Anything interesting?"

"It could be something and nothing," Penny said. "He claimed he had lost touch completely with Alec, but that Alec had called him out of the blue on Friday night. He was also surprised to hear that Alec was a 'pillar of the community' which is just something I said to, um, well, you know. But he seemed to know that Alec was a recluse, which was odd, if he hadn't had any contact with him. And he said that Alec hadn't called him for a chat, anyway. He had wanted to get in touch with Carl's ex-wife, Amanda. Except, of course, you know we tried to look her up? I know why we couldn't!" She paused, waiting in triumph for Cath to ask her what the big secret was.

Cath nodded. "Yeah, because she's called Mandy Jones now."

Penny deflated. She kicked her boot against the bench leg. "Ca-ath!" she whined like a petulant teenager. "That was *my* news."

"I guessed as much. Sorry. Not sorry."

"Good cake, by the way," Penny said. "He seemed awfully keen to get us interested in this Mandy Jones. Francine tried looking her up online last night, but we didn't find anything."

"And that's the thing," Cath said. "He turned up at the station to tell us all about Mandy, or Amanda, or whoever she is. I think maybe you spooked him. You're right. He was *very* keen to get us to look at her. Maybe he's being all public-spirited, or maybe he's an angry and bitter divorced man."

"He'd be right to be bitter, though. I mean, she did ten years in prison, didn't she?"

"So she did. And no wrong-doing before or since."

"That we know of."

Cath smiled. "I haven't met her so I'm not going to prejudge her on what might have been one stupid mistake."

"What, taking part in a robbery with a notorious gang of jewel thieves? That doesn't just happen."

"She claimed innocence all the way through the trial."

Penny shrugged. "So? Where is she now, and what does she do?"

"She's in Lincoln." Cath couldn't stop her smile getting

wider. "Fancy a visit this afternoon?"

* * * *

Cath refused the lift as a pillion passenger on the back of Penny's motorbike. She outlined brief directions and headed off for her car, while Penny went to collect the M21. She managed to catch up with Cath's car and follow her out of the old Bailgate area, and to a grey and boxy housing estate on the edge of town. Much of it was social housing, a few decades old, and three blocks of flats rose up, tall yet still dwarfed by the Cathedral on the hill. Penny parked up next to Cath in a general visitors' parking area, and looked around.

"Will my bike be safe here?"

"As safe as anywhere. Don't worry. This isn't inner city London."

"I liked inner city London. It was vibrant. I suppose I'm just unfamiliar with this area…"

"Do you want to put your gear in my car?"

"Please." Penny offloaded her heavy jacket and helmet, and followed Cath into the entrance hall of a squat building.

There was an intercom entrance for the residents, but it was propped open with a fire extinguisher. A handwritten sign on the door read, "If U nicked my trainers UR dead" to which some wag had appended "No I'm clearly not. Your trainers are great. Thanks." There was, sadly, no more room for the conversation to continue on that sheet of paper.

"Is this a shoe-stealing sort of place?" Penny asked.

"Only if you leave expensive shoes outside, I would have thought. Right, we need to be upstairs, top floor. I bet the lift isn't working."

It was, but it smelled of pee, so they took the stairs anyway.

The door to the flat was at the far end. It had a small, traditional brown mat outside that said "Welcome" and a door knocker in the shape of a comedy cat. Cath rapped the tail against the cat's bottom, and stepped back as they waited.

The door opened on a security chain, and a dark eye peered out at them. "Hello."

Cath flashed her police identification card, and introduced themselves. "Are you Amanda Jones, once Amanda Fredericks?"

"Yes."

"May we come in?"

The woman sighed heavily. She slipped the chain free, and opened the door somewhat reluctantly. She was short, and quite thick-set, with curled grey hair and a monochromatic outfit of black trousers and a thin, polyester white blouse. She led them wordlessly into the main room of the flat, which was surprisingly large with windows one two walls, and it was incredibly neat and tidy. It was a place that was crying out for doilies.

She waved them to a large sofa, and took her own place in an armchair opposite, and folded her hands on her lap. She looked old, her lined face and baggy eyes suggesting seventy and not the sixty that they knew her to be. She was very changed from the photographs of her at forty years old.

But her smile was both tired and serene. "What can I do for you, officers?"

Penny wondered if she ought to correct the mistake. Wasn't impersonating a police officer an offence?

Cath seemed to ignore it. She said, "Do you already know why we're here, Ms Jones?"

"Call me Mandy. I suspect it's to do with Alec, isn't it? I saw the news. I was shocked."

"Do you work, Mandy?" Cath asked.

Penny realised that Cath was practised at questioning people, and she decided she could learn a lot from staying silent and watching.

Mandy nodded. "Yes. I work in a shop on the High Street. We sell cards and party things."

"Have you worked there long?"

"About eight years." Mandy's hands remained in her lap, but the fingers twisted around each other. She kept her body very, very still. "Is this to do with Alec Goodwin? Or … something else?"

"What else?"

Mandy's eyes widened and then narrowed, an almost imperceptible movement. "To do with the shop," she said. "But we haven't had any shoplifters – that we're aware of – since April. And he was caught."

"No." Cath shook her head and her voice was light and kindly. "No, it's nothing to do with the shop. It is to do with Alec. You were old friends, weren't you?"

"We knew each other but it was a long time ago."

"Can you tell me about Alec? How did you know him?"

Mandy looked down for a moment. She stared at her hands. Eventually, she said, "Well. That wasn't a good time for me, and I don't like to think about it." Her voice was clearly wobbling. "I knew Alec because he was my ex-husband's best friend. I got married late in life, you see. I was thirty-five."

That's not late, thought Penny. *I've never got around to it and I'm way past thirty-five. Not that I'm ruling it out. There's a few years left in me* ... she forced her concentration back onto the scene in front of her, and held her tongue. Cath stayed silent too, waiting for Mandy to fill in the gaps.

"Anyway. Alec was our best man. They were close, my husband and Alec. But they lost touch, and anyway, I'm divorced now."

"What was your husband's name?"

"Carl Fredericks. He runs a bulb business. I have his contact details if you want. We do still send Christmas cards to each other, that kind of thing. It's not a friendship, I suppose, but it's as good as it could be."

Penny kept her face carefully blank. It didn't match with what Carl had said. He'd claimed to have no contact

185

with Mandy these days.

Mandy started to get to her feet, but Cath waved her back down. "It's okay. We've had a chat with him already. When did you divorce?"

"Ten years ago."

"So you moved here…?"

"Yes."

"And got the job in the card shop…?"

"After a year or two."

"What were you doing before?"

Mandy hesitated. "I was unemployed."

You were in prison, Penny thought. *But a more unlikely looking criminal I have never seen. It must have really changed her.*

Cath let the matter drop. "Times were tough, eh?"

"Yes." Mandy was looking down again, and she must have known that she looked suspicious. She began speaking, all in a rush. "Look. It didn't work out with me and Carl. Sometimes, things don't. It was my fault. Totally my fault. I … I'm not proud of this, but I had a gambling problem. These days, I'm clean. I go to meetings and I help others, which is why I'm speaking out about it now, because I have to own up to it. It wasn't a good time for me, or for Carl.

And that's that."

Oh, thought Penny, *that is not what I expected to hear.* Cath was nodding in sympathy.

"Of course, of course," Cath said soothingly. "Thank you for being honest with us."

Mandy didn't raise her head. "Gambling … it destroyed me and it destroyed my marriage. Everything went wrong. Everything." Finally she flung her head back, and her eyes were glistening with tears. "I am so lucky to have come through it all," she said, a sudden fierce passion in her voice. "Now, I have this flat, I have a job, and I have friends. I am blessed to have been given a second chance. Not everyone gets this kind of chance. I feel I have to make the very best of my remaining time on earth."

Penny shivered. The conviction in Mandy's voice seemed real and raw. If she was lying, she was very convincing. Penny stole a sideways glance at Cath, who was looking carefully neutral.

"Thank you, Mandy. I can see this isn't easy for you," Cath said. And then she was silent again, leaving a large gap in the conversation.

It stretched out. Penny felt uncomfortable but she

knew what Cath was doing, and she bit her own tongue until Mandy spoke again.

"There's something I haven't told you. I haven't told anyone."

"Go on."

Mandy was hiding her face again. "Carl called me. Right out of the blue, he rang me. Although like I said, we send each other cards and that, we don't really socialise together. But he rang me up on … uh, Saturday night, just over a week ago. I had been at work, you see. So he rang me that evening and told me that Alec wanted to get in touch."

"So you had lost touch with Alec, and he didn't have your contact details?"

"That's right. He'd gone to Carl, apparently, to try and find me. And Carl rang me to warn me."

"*Warn* you?"

Mandy rushed on, her fingers now twisting frantically like snakes. "But I said, I said to him, to Carl, it was all okay. You know? It was all water under the bridge, and I had forgiven Alec. It didn't matter."

"Forgiven him for what?"

She leaped to her feet, and rubbed her face. "Excuse

me. It was all such a bad time. The past …" She dashed out of the room, and they heard running water.

Penny and Cath exchanged looks. Penny shrugged and Cath frowned, but nodded. She stood up and Penny followed. When Mandy came back in, Cath thrust out her hand.

"Thank you so much for your time, Ms Jones. We really appreciate this, and I must apologise for any distress we might have caused you. If you remember anything about Alec, please do pop into the station for an informal chat. Any information could be extremely valuable in finding this killer. Here's my card." She passed over a small, discreet rectangle. "And please, when you feel ready to talk about Carl Fredericks, we would be very willing to listen." Cath stared meaningfully at Mandy, and she reddened, and looked away.

They left, and Penny managed to stay quiet until they were out in the parking area again.

"She had more to tell us!" Penny exploded. "We should have stayed and got it out of her?"

"What do you suggest?" Cath asked. "Thumbscrews?"

"Well, no, of course not. Not actual thumbscrews. But

the verbal equivalent, yes."

"I don't think information that we pressed out of her would have been reliable," Cath said. "Yes, she's hiding something. But what we need to do now is to find the loose threads. We need to tweak the ends of what she's hiding, and then go back to her. If we know more than we do at the moment, we have something to bargain with."

"We do know more," Penny argued. "We know she did ten years in prison! She didn't tell us that, did she?"

"Of course not. Who would? And she certainly alluded to it, with saying she's moved on. Knowing what we know, we could read between the lines there."

"I still think we've missed something."

"I *know* we have," Cath said crossly, "but we can't just blunder forward without thinking it over."

"But that's what I'm best at! I'm great at blundering. It's my top skill."

Cath rolled her eyes. "And don't we know it." She sighed and opened her car door, and ferreted about for a bottle of water. She grimaced as she took a swig. "Warm water. Lovely. Did anything else strike you as odd, though?"

"Yes, absolutely. Carl Fredericks told us yesterday that

he had no contact with Mandy and he didn't have her address or phone number."

"He said much the same to us. He certainly didn't mention any phone call. I wonder what he was 'warning' her about?"

"You see!" Penny said. "We should have stayed and asked more!"

"She was clamming up and she was getting upset. She would have said anything. Let's go gently and gain her trust. I am also going to ask around the local gamblers' help groups. They are anonymous, and I would not break that sanctity, but I can do a little careful poking."

"And the other thing," Penny said, pulled her helmet out of the back seat of Cath's car. "I wonder what she meant when she said she'd *forgiven* Alec?"

Chapter Fourteen

Penny took the direct route home that Monday afternoon. She didn't realise that she was eager to get back and talk to Francine until she barged into her own hallway and found the cottage empty, and felt a strange and sinking disappointment that took her quite by surprise.

Kali was sunning herself in the front room, wriggling over a few inches every half hour to stay in the last patch of sunlight as it tracked across the floor. She looked up as Penny entered, and thumped her tail on the floor, but didn't relinquish her sunbathing. Penny shook her head at her, and knelt down for a quick fuss.

Her knees protested almost immediately. With a groan she staggered up and went to make a cup of tea.

* * * *

She devoted Tuesday to work. She was woefully behind on her arts and crafts, and only broke off to walk the dog in the morning. She had emails to answer, her website to monitor, and a handful of sales from her online shop that needed parcelling and posting.

She spent the afternoon gradually relaxing back into her old routine of experimentation and hard graft. She had picked up some floral fabric many weeks previously. She was a sucker for anything fabric or fibre related, and had to ration herself to how much she could spend in a haberdashery. She had avoided a yarn shop that day, but ended up in a charity shop instead, and impulsively bought a large cotton sheet with an old-fashioned paisley pattern on it. Since then, it had lingered in her stash with all the other guilt-inducing purchases.

Now she tried a little complementary embroidery in metallic thread that wove around the printed tendrils. In her head, it looked great.

In practise, less so.

However, she was absorbed in the work, even though she spent as much time ripping it out and starting again. It had been too long since she had lost herself in craft, she reflected. It was like an active meditation and the hours flew by.

Francine had gone out, and then returned, passing through the kitchen to grab a drink before sitting out in the back garden with a book. Kali wandered through from time to time. With the kitchen door propped open, Penny could hear a distant radio, and an occasional aeroplane passed over to temporarily mute the bees in the flowers.

If this wasn't peace, then it was certainly pretty close to it.

* * * *

Francine seemed quiet and didn't want to accompany Penny to the progress meeting for the Sculpture Trail that Tuesday evening. She murmured something about a headache, and took herself off to her room.

Her room! Penny smiled to herself. She wanted Francine to leave, but she knew now that she was going to miss her when she went.

The community hall was packed, even more so than

the previous meeting. Perhaps people were hoping for more shock announcements, but Penny hoped fervently that they were to be disappointed. She stepped into the throng and was immediately beset from all sides.

"Who did it, then?" was the general question. "You're in cahoots with the police. Who's a suspect?" This was invariably followed by the questioner's list of potential murderers, which in one case included the prime minister and a random milkman in Lincoln.

Penny smiled and waved them all away, trying to listen to the hints and clues in what people offered. But how could she tell what was gold-class information, and what was the product of a fevered imagination, too many mystery novels, and a grudge against a neighbour who once had a bonfire while their washing was on the line?

The only member from the town council present was the short, loud butcher, Shaun Kapowski. He stood at the table on the raised platform, next to Steve. In spite of being a good foot shorter than Steve, the council leader looked larger. *It was the confident way he stood,* Penny thought. *Anyone who wrestled dead cows and large knives for a living was bound to stand with confidence.*

Shaun's booming voice called the audience to take their seats. There weren't enough chairs, and people stood in ranks along the sides of the hall. Eventually the chatter died down, and every pair of eyes in the place was fixed on the two figures.

Penny had managed to get a seat next to a man she didn't know, but a few rows in front she could see Agatha's wobbling black beehive. Someone else prodded her between the shoulder blades, and she turned to see Sheila and her husband from the Post Office. She nodded hi, and returned her attention to the silent pair on the dais.

In contrast to Shaun's easy assurance, poor Steve looked like a terrified sheep. He hunched his shoulders, making him look more like a teenager with his lank hair hanging loose. He shifted from foot to foot.

As he was about to speak, there was a murmur from the back of the hall, and a few people turned around. Steve's mouth opened and closed.

"It's Ginni," someone said, and Penny craned her neck around too. She could just make out the tall figure of the local florist standing at the back.

"We are here to discuss the progress of the Sculpture

Trail." Shaun's voice brought everyone's attention back once more. "Since the sad and untimely death of our Alec Goodwin, Steve Llewellyn has most kindly stepped forward to continue his legacy and ensure that our town can unveil the Trail at our August Fair."

That was a matter of weeks away. Penny folded her arms and studied Steve. He did not look comfortable.

Shaun reached up with his hand and clapped Steve on the upper arm. "And Steve is here to tell us all about how it's going! Over to you, young man. You're doing a sterling job. Well done."

If Penny closed her eyes, Shaun's voice put her in mind of a retired Colonel from a 1950's film. Who said "sterling" these days? When she opened her eyes again, Shaun had sat down, and Steve was left floundering, alone.

He stared at the table in front of him, and mumbled, "Hi everyone. Yeah. So we're doing some tiles for the poles and it will be finished by the fair."

There was a pause.

And then everyone in the hall wanted to ask a question. Hands waved, and people shouted things out. In the midst of the cacophony, Shaun rose to his feet and yelled for quiet. Then he began taking questions one by one.

The first questioner asked, "Why aren't you doing what Alec planned? He was having carved wooden poles, none of this tiles business."

Steve's voice was rough and cracked. He coughed to clear his throat but it didn't help. "I thought we should do something a bit different. I didn't want to take another artist's vision. Felt a bit wrong, didn't it? And I am good in clay and that."

"How many are you making?"

"There will be twelve in total. I done about five."

"Are these clay tiles?"

Penny recognised Mary's voice. It was a sensible question, and one she herself had worried about since she heard of Steve's plans.

"Yeah, they are."

"But won't they get weathered?" More than one person spoke at a time, and there was a murmur of consternation.

"It's kiln-fired stoneware, isn't it," Steve said, flatly, not as a question. "And you can put a sealer on the inside and paint the outside with acrylic and it will be all right, so…"

"Nah," a man shouted out without Shaun's intervention. "Water will still get in, and then it will freeze, and the ice expands and boom! It all shatters. Happened to my terracotta pots. I had them on my patio one winter. They–"

"This *isn't* terracotta," Steve said, his voice louder now. "I told you. It's *stoneware*. All right?"

"Don't you get shirty with me, young man!" the questioner retorted, getting to his feet.

"Yeah but you don't understand pottery, do you?"

More people shouted out, and a few others started to stand up. It unleashed a wave of people having to move to retain their view of the platform. "So what's on the designs of these tiles, then?" someone called out.

Steve tried to answer but someone else was speaking now. "Carved poles, that's what we want. It's tactile."

"We need to see your designs. Come on, where are your designs?"

Shaun was frantically calling for quiet. Steve, however, jumped onto a chair and then up onto the table, and the audience was shocked enough to finally shut up. Everyone was standing now, even Penny, who had moved to the side for a better view.

"I'm the artist, all right?"

Oh goodness, oh no, Penny thought. She pleaded internally with Steve. *Don't do this. Don't go on like I think you're going to go on...*

But he did.

"Stoneware is weather proof! I can't use Alec Goodwin's designs! I got asked to do this! And I'm doing it! You don't know what you're talking about. Which is why YOU are not doing it!"

His tirade was aimed at that one questioner, and everyone else in the room. His face was red and sweaty and he had balled his fists, swinging his long arms menacingly.

"Get down!" Shaun reached up and pulled at the leg of Steve's jeans, but he shook the little butcher away. "Get down, lad!"

"I am the *artist!*" Steve shouted, focusing on Shaun this time. "Don't you people understand?"

Penny was cringing openly by this point. *Shut up, shut up, you fool,* she thought, trying to will some psychic connection to open up between her and the irrational idiot on the table.

The hall was erupting now.

"Us?"

"You people?"

"What are you on, boy?"

"I know about terracotta, I do!"

"Arrogant little–"

Penny thought she couldn't get any more embarrassed for Steve, but then Shaun climbed onto a chair to get a better grip on Steve to haul him down. With the butcher's great strength, Steve was bound to come off worse. It was turning into a farce.

Steve flung his arm out to the side, knocking Shaun backwards, so he had to jump off the chair to retain his balance. Then Steve leaped to the floor. Without looking at anyone, he simply ran out of the hall, shouting, "I'm the artist! You're all the same. Just like uni. I–"

And he was gone.

For a moment, one bare brief second, there was a silence, taut and charged with the coming explosion.

And then, as one, everyone turned to their neighbour and began to dissect everything they had just witnessed.

Poor, poor Steve, Penny thought. *What a complete numpty.*

But then, maybe Shaun should not have put such a young and immature man under the spotlight so publically.

She felt so acutely bad for the spectacle that Steve had displayed that she wanted to get out of the hall. People were gossiping and analysing and speculating and it made her feel uncomfortable. She caught, out of the corner of her eye, the sight of Agatha milling around and decided she needed to leave before she was cornered.

Not many others were going. She pushed her way through the crowd, toward the exit at the front of the hall.

Ginni was standing on the front steps, staring down the road at the retreating figure of her nephew.

"Ginni, I just want to say that I'm so—"

Penny didn't get to finish her sentence. All she wanted to say was that she felt sorry for Steve. But Ginni whirled around, her reddened eyes narrowed.

"Don't," she hissed, and turned away, presenting a broad padded shoulder.

Penny swallowed her words, and passed by quickly.

* * * *

She walked south out of town. She wanted to talk to Barry again, but this time, not about Alec.

Barry and Steve had been drinking together on the night that Alec had died. Barry and Steve, Steve and Barry; any which way that she put the pairing together, it didn't make sense to her. Barry was nearly ten years older than Steve. They weren't typical friends. As one grew older, she had found that age differences between friends mattered less, but when you were in your early twenties, it seemed to count for more.

Barry was a labourer. Steve was a university graduate.

They were both local, though. As Drew had often pointed out to her, she wasn't aware of the family links and connections that the more settled residents took for granted. So perhaps there was something she was missing.

As she walked, she remembered something that Francine had told her. She'd seen Steve act in a volatile and over-the-top manner in the market. At the time, Penny had dismissed it.

Maybe Steve really was a hot-head. He couldn't control himself; he had issues. It now looked likely.

The tape was totally gone from the entrance to Alec's property. She crunched up the gravel drive and had only got halfway before she was beset by the two Staffies. The squat, broad-chested dogs thundered towards her, mouths open in wide daft grins.

"Hey, Bob. Hey, Cassandra. What have I got for you?" Penny found some stray kibble in her pockets and threw a scattering to the dogs, who leapt upon the dry food eagerly.

"What you feeding to my dogs? Bribery, is it, ha ha?"

"Hi, Barry." Penny hadn't noticed him at first. He was standing in his garden with a can of beer in his hand. His white vest was grubby, and he was wearing shabby shorts. By his feet was a pile of weeds, and a wheelbarrow lay on the rough lawn behind him.

"Hi. You came round before, didn't you, with that other one?"

"Yeah. I'm Penny."

"I remember."

"Doing some gardening?"

"If you can call it that, yeah. I ain't much for it, like, but I do a bit. I ain't too sure what are weeds and what are plants, though. Have you come to see me, or me dogs, then?"

"Oh, the dogs, definitely." Penny crouched down and fussed both dogs for a short while.

"Well, they are better company than me, ha ha."

She stayed petting the dogs, but looked up at him. He clutched his can of beer to his belly like a talisman. "Barry, I wanted to talk to you about Steve."

His eyebrows shot up. "I thought you was going to say Alec."

She shook her head. "We spoke about Alec last time. I know you didn't get on, and I'm not going to bother you about him. No." She drew in a deep breath. "You'll hear about this soon enough, anyway, but Steve has had a bit of a meltdown in the public meeting about the Sculpture Trail."

"What, just now, like?"

"Yeah. He got very angry and ran off."

"Where?"

"I don't know. And anyway, I thought, as a friend of his, you would want to know."

Barry rolled his beer can between his hands but didn't say anything.

Penny tickled one of the dogs under the chin, and he

rolled over to present his belly for a rub. "Is this one Bob?"

"Yup."

She obliged Bob's demands, and said, "You and Steve are friends, aren't you? I hope I haven't got the wrong end of the stick."

"Nah, he's an all right sort of kid, yeah. Yeah, your next question is gonna be, was he here that night Alec was killed? Yes, he was. I already told the police that. We were chilling out with a few drinks and that."

"Right. And does he tend to fly off the handle quite quickly, usually?"

Barry shrugged. "Couldn't say. It's not like I ever pushed him to get angry, is it?"

"Is the Sculpture Trail causing him a lot of stress? People do react strangely when they're worried."

Barry shrugged again. "Nah, still couldn't say. We never talked about it."

"Right." Penny waited.

"I reckon, though, if he were stressed and all, it were probably more to do with uni and his family and all that."

Bingo, thought Penny. She tried not to sound too eager for more information. *Play it cool*, she reminded herself. *Like*

Cath would. "Oh? I imagine, then, he's glad to have finished his studies."

"Finished," Barry said, "but not completed."

"I beg your pardon?" Penny's hand was still, now, on Bob's round belly and he was squirming around on his back to encourage her to continue. She ignored him. "Do you mean…"

Barry looked away into the middle distance. "Ah, I shouldn't have said anything, and that. But yeah. He never did graduate and that's gonna be on his mind, because no one else knows about that. Keep it under your hat, eh? Don't you be letting on that I said anything. Or I'll set Bob on you, ha ha."

"And he is truly a ferocious beast," Penny acknowledged as the little bull terrier got to his feet and shook himself all over. "Don't worry. My lips are sealed. It explains a lot about Steve, though. I do feel for him. He's not finding all this very easy, is he?"

"Nope, he ain't. People need to get off his back a bit."

Penny stood up and massaged her knees. "He doesn't do himself any favours by flying off the handle, though. You might want to chat to him about that."

208

"Maybe. We just talk about dogs and stuff, really. Man stuff."

Penny rolled her eyes at him but he shrugged at her, and took a swig of his beer. "Well, I'll let you get on with your gardening. Thank you for talking to me, though."

"S'all right. Don't see a right lot of folks down this end. Mostly scared off by Alec, and now by Alec's ghost no doubt. It would be just like the miserable old so-and-so to linger around like a spirit, ha ha."

"You don't miss him much, then?"

"Nah," Barry said. Suddenly a thought occurred to him. "Hey, I ain't a suspect, am I?"

"You'd have to ask the police that," Penny said. She thought, *is he a suspect? He can't be ruled out.*

"What about Steve? Cos he was here with me, wasn't he? We're abil ... alibs for each other."

"Alibis, yes. I don't know if either you or Steve are suspects. But neither of you have been arrested," she added, "so that's a good sign, right?"

"Hmm." Barry rubbed Bob's head and then looked around for Cassandra, who was busy dragging the careful pile of weeds to pieces. "Yeah, I guess so."

Penny waved goodbye and walked home, thoughtfully.

Was Barry really a serious suspect?

And Steve?

She was growing ever more suspicious of Steve Llewellyn.

Chapter Fifteen

On Wednesday morning, Penny took Kali out for a walk through town. Kali's reactions to other dogs were so much better, but Penny still went out armed with lots of tasty treats to keep Kali conditioned to the idea that other dogs meant yummy food was going to happen. She decided to take her through town because it was good for the dog to visit new places, or places she hadn't been to for a while. They turned left at the crossroads and headed north towards some new estates, and then doubled back and along a street that ran parallel to the High Street. She came out on the other end of town, and began to work back to the centre again.

She passed by the industrial units where Drew still had his blacksmith's workshop. He had said that he'd keep it on for a while, as he had enjoyed ornamental ironwork as a hobby. She wondered if he had finally let it go yet. He was so busy with work.

Next to that was the old fuel station and car repair place, Alf's Garage. She'd never been to it. The petrol was far cheaper at the larger petrol station on the roundabout to the north of town where the bypass swung around. It was open twenty-four hours and was a national chain. Alf's, by contrast, was a run-down concrete structure with two pumps and a ramshackle shed on the side which claimed to offer bargain MOTs.

There was also a hosepipe which declared itself, somewhat optimistically, to be a car wash. There was a white van being cleaned, and when she caught a glimpse of ragged hair as the man bent down on the far side, she slowed her pace.

Yes, it was Steve. The van was plain white but the rear doors had a small floral design and a phone number painted on them.

Kali strained forward, her tail wagging. She was keen on water. She was keen, that is, on trying to bite water. She would spend all day chasing a hose pipe if you let her. Penny wasn't sure if it was healthy, or some strange doggy obsessive disorder.

Steve stood up and saw them looking at him. He snarled and began to turn away. Penny made a snap decision, and dropped Kali's lead.

The over-enthusiastic dog bounded over to Steve, all flapping ears and flailing tail and foaming mouth, launching herself at the end of the hosepipe.

"Oh no!" Penny said with all the fake horror of a 1960's B-movie. "Kali, come back!"

Kali had no intention of coming back, especially as her finely tuned ears knew the difference between the sound of a strict order and the more usual conversational stream of words that she generally ignored, filtering only for the word "food" hidden in there.

Steve turned the hose so that the jet of water was directed at the floor, rather than hit the dog. Kali thought he was playing with her, and pounced on the bubbling stream, immediately getting soaked through. Steve was horrified.

"It's not my fault," he began saying as Penny reached the scene of watery devastation.

"I know, I know. Totally my fault. Don't worry. She

loves water. Don't you, you big monkey, hey, hey?"

"You let go," Steve said. He still sounded belligerent and Penny knew he was simply expecting a fight.

He assumed he was going to be blamed, she thought.

"I did. She is so strong! Well, never mind. She's happy now. I'm sorry she disturbed you. She didn't scare you, did she?"

Steve grimaced. "No. I wouldn't be scared of no dog."

"That's good. Yes, I can see you're a dog person." She could see nothing of the sort. He was staring at them both, unsmiling. She continued, in a light and friendly tone, "You know, it's amazing how many people are scared of dogs! Especially with the way Kali looks. People cross the road when I come along. It's such a shame."

"Yeah."

"She just wants to play with you. Go on, wiggle the hosepipe." *I will get a smile out of you yet, you miserable boy*, she thought. *No one can watch a sopping-wet dog play with water and not smile, right?*

Steve jerked the hosepipe slightly and Kali pounced, pawing and biting at the water. When she looked up at them, her expression was comical, with her wet matted fur,

214

drooping ears and lolling tongue.

"She'll stink your house out now," Steve said.

"I'm used to it."

"Right." He splashed a little more water around and the dog responded with an enthusiastic wag of her tail as she chased and pawed.

"Are you doing a little bit of work for your aunt?" Penny asked while he was half-distracted.

"What? Oh, yeah. She doesn't half obsess about this van being spotless. She reckons it reflects on her business. I think I clean it every other day."

"Are you helping in the shop, too?"

"Nah. Flowers ain't my thing. I've got other things to do."

"Such as the Sculpture Trail?" Penny asked.

Steve snorted and Kali looked up in surprise in case she'd done something wrong. He was more in tune than Penny had anticipated. He apologised to the dog, and flicked more water her way. "All sorts of stuff," he said. "I've got the rest of my life to plan, you know."

"Yes. I remember what it was like when I finished at university. I'd studied art, like you. I was full of these ideas that I'd live in Paris or Mexico or somewhere and eat strange foods and continue my hedonistic student lifestyle. I was going to change the world!"

"Yeah, and did you?"

"Nope. I did get a good job with a television production company. Well, I say good … I was at the bottom of the heap, and it was long hours for low pay, but it was in London and I met some amazing people, and I worked hard. And I progressed. The problem was, though, I ended up doing about twenty-five years of working up the corporate ladder and I realised last year that none of it had been my original aim. That's why I gave it all up to come here."

"Oh, I get it. You realised you'd sold out."

She thought about arguing back, but in spite of his aggressive tone, she had to acknowledge that he was correct. So she said, mildly, "Yes. And I did something about it. I made a change. Life doesn't turn out like you expect, but if you're flexible and roll with it, it can still be quite exciting."

"Yeah, living here in the middle of nowhere. Wow. Too much excitement." Steve's shoulders were rounded and he looked sullen, but he kept on playing with the dog.

"So what's next?"

"I dunno."

She couldn't betray Barry's confidence in her, but she took a chance at asking what she hoped was an innocent-sounding and logical question. "What did you come out with, in the end? Was it a degree, or a BTec perhaps?"

The hosepipe stopped moving. Staring at the floor, Steve growled out, "It weren't nothing."

"Have you not finished yet? Lots of people take a year out. It's really useful."

"Oh, yeah, I've finished all right. I got nothing. I didn't even bother submitting my final dissertation. They pretty much asked me to leave. They told me there were no point carrying on. So there you go. You asked. What am I going to do, hey?"

"I am sorry to hear that you had a bad time. I think you're right in coming here to relax and get your head straight about your future. Just give it some time, Steve. You'll find a way forward. Having a degree isn't the be-all and end-all, you know."

"You can say that cos you've got one."

Penny nodded. "Perhaps. Does your aunt know?"

"What, that I'm a scummy drop-out? No. Nor me mum or me dad."

"You'll need to tell them. It's July. Won't they be expecting to go to your graduation soon?"

He shrugged. "I told them I didn't want no fuss."

"Oh, Steve. Well, you know your family best, and you're an adult now. Take your time. It will all work out. I know that sounds like a silly platitude but honestly, I mean it."

"Yeah, thanks." He said it in the same tone that a teenager would mutter out "whatever." He started to direct the hose back onto the van again, and Penny called Kali to her. The soaking dog bounded over, lead still trailing behind, and shook herself when she was in close range.

"I know that was deliberate, you little pest!" Penny said, picking up the wet lead. "Come on, you. Let's get home. Oh – hi, Ginni."

Once again, the hose's jet of water hit the floor as Steve stood frozen in shock.

Ginni's gaze flickered from Steve to Penny and back to Steve. She was dressed, as usual, in a severe power suit. She looked as if she'd taken her style inspiration from female politicians in the 1980's and had not seen any need to update since then. With her tall figure and already broad shoulders that hardly needed a set of shoulder pads, she was the epitome of Amazonian. *Corporate Amazonian*, Penny thought. *A whole new terrifying trend.*

"Steve. I wanted to see how you were doing. You have been quite a while," she said to Steve. "Hello, Penny. How are you?"

Penny could feel the stiff politeness in every syllable. "Fine, thank you. And yourself?"

Ginni was clearly not fine. She said, "I'm very well, thank you. Steve, are you nearly done? I need to deliver some floral displays."

"Yeah, sorry. I was distracted." He shot Penny an accusatory look.

"Yes, my fault entirely," she said to Ginni. "I am so sorry."

"Gossiping?" Ginni said. She tried to frown but she just looked rather sad and tired. In a strange way, that made Penny feel sorry for her. It was hard to see a woman of such strength seem vulnerable.

"No, not at all," Penny said firmly. "In fact, we were

talking about university. Did you know I did an art degree?"

Penny's intention was to deflect the focus onto herself, but it didn't work. Steve was feeling too sensitive about his own position and he had not yet learned to hide his feelings. He growled and stamped over to the tap, turning the hose off with a wrench. From inside the repair workshop, a man shouted, "About time! That's our water bill, bor!"

He might have meant the Lincolnshire slang of "neighbour" or just "young boy" but either way, Steve resented it. He turned so that the man could not see him, before flicking a rude gesture his way.

"Steven!" Ginni admonished. "And if you must be so offensive, at least have the courage to do it to his face."

Penny bit her smile back. She agreed with Ginni on that one.

"Yeah," Steve said, randomly. He rolled up the hosepipe and came back over to the van with a chamois cloth to do the final polish. "Whatevs. I won't be long."

Ginni pointedly looked at her watch and then folded her arms. She was making it clear she was staying. She nodded at Penny. "Art, was it? And you got a good job afterwards, didn't you?"

"I did, yes, eventually. I started at the bottom and worked up. In truth, I think my attitude was more important than my degree." She hoped Steve would take that on board.

"A good degree makes all the difference," Ginni said. "It was a chance I was never able to take. One can only hope that others make the most of their opportunities. Sadly some people seem to lack the serious approach they need. Steve hasn't even told me what result he got."

Penny's stomach tightened. She knew there was a sickening inevitability about the coming revelation and Steve would forever blame her for it.

And here it came.

"Well, I'll tell you what result I got, seeing as you all seem so blinking keen to get it out of me," Steve said, adding a muttered swearword which caused Ginni to hiss, and Steve to colour up red.

"Please do," Ginni said tightly.

Penny began to back away, clicking her tongue discreetly to tempt Kali away from the really, really interesting smell of Ginni's shoes.

She hadn't got far enough when Steve blurted out, "I failed, all right? Actually, no, I didn't even get the chance to fail."

"Come on, Kali…"

"I was kicked out! Yeah, there you go. Happy now?"

"Kali!"

Finally the dog appeared to notice the increasing pressure on the lead, and sprang over to Penny, all big eyes and wagging tail.

Ginni and Steve were facing one another, and Ginni looked shocked. Steve was red in the face, and quite upset. Neither glanced at Penny. She waved goodbye anyway, because it felt like the right thing to do, and then turned around to walk briskly away.

Steve had an awful lot of explaining to do.

* * * *

Penny found herself doing an awful lot of explaining, too. Francine was eager to hear all about the latest revelations.

"I don't see what the fuss was about," Penny said.

Francine shook her head. "I do. Poor Steve. I bet he was the first in his family to go to university, wasn't he?"

"I got that impression."

"So much expectation riding on him! Of course he's

going to lie."

"Silly boy," Penny said. "People do the daftest things."

"Don't we just."

They both laughed. Then Penny said, "Have you any plans for this afternoon?"

"Why?"

"I'm going over to Sleaford to the crafts hub there. They've got a new exhibition about wool. Do you fancy it?"

Francine smiled. "No, but thank you. I'm making plans to move on … you'll be glad to know."

"Oh? Gosh. What sort of plans?"

"Nothing definite yet. I don't want to jinx anything before it's sorted…"

"Of course, of course. Are you staying in today though?"

"Yes. And don't worry. I'll look after Kali."

"Thanks."

* * * *

In spite of Penny researching which mobile phone network provider gave the best coverage in Lincolnshire, she still encountered blackspots where there was no signal. She had been assured it was common in the rural areas and that she simply had to deal with it. Coming from London, where you could use the free wi-fi of every other business on the street, never mind actual phone coverage, it was a shock to the system.

She was getting used to the phenomena of her phone being silent for many hours, and then suddenly bursting into life with a backlog of text messages and missed calls. So it was as she left the delightful provincial exhibition and made her way back to where she'd parked her car. Her phone buzzed three times in quick succession. She waited until she was sitting in the driver's seat until she thumbed the phone and viewed the missed calls.

All three were from Francine, and there was a voicemail and a text message.

She couldn't help thinking the worst.

And the worst was confirmed. The text simply said, "Call me as soon as you can."

The voicemail was a little more explanatory. "Don't panic!" But Francine's voice was high and strained. "It's Kali. She's going to be okay but I'm at an emergency vet in

Lincoln." She rattled off the name and address. "Call me when you can."

Frantically, Penny rang Francine's mobile phone and her hands were sweating and shaking by the time Francine answered.

"What happened?" Penny demanded.

"It's okay, she's going to be all right. The vet has had to make her be sick. It looks like she ate something she shouldn't have eaten."

"What? What did you feed her?"

"I haven't fed her anything! It wasn't her meal time. We were sitting in the garden. Well, I was in and out. And then she went funny … and I called the vet and brought her in."

"I'm on my way." Penny threw the phone onto the passenger seat and slammed the car into gear, managing an impressive wheel-spin out of the car park and onto the road.

She drove as quickly as she dared on the treacherous Lincolnshire roads, and it felt painfully slow. She knew, roughly, where the emergency vet surgery was located, and only took two infuriating wrong turns to reach it. Then she was out of the car, and flinging herself into the reception area, where she fell over a mop being wielded by a woman in a burgundy polo shirt.

Francine was on her feet and at her side immediately.

"Mind the wee," the woman said, moving her bucket. "We had an excited terrier in just now."

Penny didn't care. "Where's Kali?"

"Ah! Are you the Rottie's owner?"

"Yes."

"It's okay," both Francine and the woman said in unison.

The woman put her bucket and mop to one side and beckoned Penny to the front desk. "She will be fine. But she ate rather a lot of something that has violently disagreed with her. Now, dogs do this a lot. Don't worry. If there is something disgusting and smelly, they'll try to ingest it. I'm sure you know that already."

"She's pretty good. Sometimes she has a good bite of some horse poo, but overall she's not bad."

"It could have been anything," the receptionist assured her. "We had a Saint Bernard in who'd got into a storeroom and eaten half a bag of onions. They are toxic to dogs, which a lot of people don't realise when they give scraps

226

from the Sunday roast."

"Was the dog okay?"

"Yes, but only due to his size. Raisins and grapes are another thing."

"Oh! Kali's eaten grapes. Oh my goodness. This is all my fault."

"When did she eat the grapes?"

"Weeks ago. I dropped some on the floor and whoosh – gone before I could pick them up."

"It's unlikely to be them, then. Some dogs can eat them and others go into kidney failure. And we don't know why."

"Oh. So what did Kali eat?"

"I don't know. The vet might have more answers for you later. If you could take a seat for a moment…"

Penny thanked her and slumped down next to Francine. "Has she dug anything up in the garden?" she asked. "Honestly, I'm not blaming you, not at all. I know you can't keep an eye on her for every minute of the day."

"I feel so bad, though," Francine said, and she was clearly close to tears. "I've been trying so hard to be her friend. There's nothing she could have eaten, I am sure of it. She was by my side most of the time, even when I left the garden and went into the kitchen. You know what she's like! If there's a chance of food, she's there. I can't think what poisoned her."

A cold chill ran down Penny's spine. "Poisoned."

"Yes. There are no onions in your garden, are there?"

"Poisoned … just like Alec …"

"No!" Francine widened her eyes. "It can't be linked. You don't think… do you?"

"I have a history of upsetting people when I go around asking questions," Penny said. "And maybe that's okay. I am fair game, if I go poking into other people's lives. But to target my dog. No! That is *not okay.*"

Francine had tears in her eyes once more. "I am so, so, so sorry," she said, and Penny knew that she meant it.

Suddenly the vet emerged from a back room. She was a slim woman with dark hair and a subtle accent that sounded vaguely European but was impossible to place. She introduced herself as Anna, which didn't narrow down the possible countries of origin particularly.

Penny tried to focus as Anna explained that Kali would stay in overnight for observation, but now the messy stuff was out of the way, they were concentrating on rehydrating her and would be checking her main functions over the next few hours.

Penny thanked her profusely, signed some forms, paid a huge wodge of cash that she didn't for a moment begrudge, and shuffled out onto the pavement. She felt bereft. She wanted to go in and see Kali, but the vet advised against it. Instead she clung to Francine and let herself have a quick moment of self-pity.

Then she pulled herself together. "Okay. Kali is in the best place she can be. I think I'm going to call in to see if Cath's at work."

"Are you sure? Don't you want to come home?"

"Not really," Penny said. "I want to distract myself from the fact that when I come home, Kali won't be there."

They hugged and Francine went off to buy some fancy and expensive food for their evening meal, and Penny made her way to Lincoln police station.

* * * *

The usual dour desk sergeant didn't even say hello. He frowned, then rolled his eyes, and waved her to a seat as he picked up the phone to call through on the internal system.

"She's here, that woman," he said.

When the security door opened and Cath stepped into the reception area, Penny said, "Your staff need a bit of training in customer service."

"We're police," the man behind the plastic screen said. "Not on the fish counter at the supermarket."

"Come on. Let's go sit outside," Cath said. "Have you any news?"

"This and that, but nothing that really amounts to anything. I would put Steve Llewellyn and Barry Neville on the list of suspects, but nothing's really certain."

"And Carl Fredericks and Mandy Jones?" Cath said. They walked a little way to a small urban park and settled under a tree, on a carved wooden bench.

"Yes. Mandy because she wasn't honest with us, and Carl because … well, he wasn't exactly straight, either."

"Tell me about Steve and Barry, though," Cath said.

Penny quickly filled her in on the latest developments. "So you see, Steve isn't telling us all the truth either, and Barry has his own issues. They could well be in it together."

"It's possible," Cath said. "But we have been moving

forward too…"

"Tell me! Goodness knows, I need something to keep my mind occupied right now." Penny outlined the problem with Kali, but downplayed the possibility that she had been deliberately targeted for Penny's involvement. It was her worst fear, and the most likely explanation, yet she felt reluctant to tell Cath and have her panic and take her off the case.

Cath picked up on something in her manner, though, and asked if she definitely wanted to stay as their unofficial investigator.

"Yes, please. Tell me about your progress."

"We called Mandy in for a formal interview," Cath said.

"Oh my goodness! I thought you were all for playing it cool and gaining her trust."

"Yes, we were," Cath explained. "But we ran background checks, of course. One thing that had interested me when we spoke to her was her reaction to us. She wondered if we were there because of her job. So we looked into her job, because she was hiding something about it. It turned out that she had lied on her application form to work in that shop. She never declared her conviction for robbery."

"Oh! What does that mean?"

"It means she's unreliable in what she tells us. And it also means she can be dismissed from her work, too."

"Poor Mandy. She should have been honest at the start."

Cath raised her eyebrows. "Really? Then she probably wouldn't have got the job at all. It's hard to find work, and even more so when you have a criminal record."

"It's so long ago now, though. It shouldn't affect her."

"The conviction is spent now, yes. But when she applied for the job, it wasn't. And that omission invalidates her entire job application and subsequent employment."

"She must have known that," Penny said.

"Oh yes. When it emerged, when we challenged her on it, she broke down completely. It was rather uncomfortable, to be honest. She knew she'd done wrong but she saw no way of ever coming clean without losing her job."

"What a lot to hide for so long. And of course…" Penny rubbed her cheek. "Alec knew, didn't he?"

"I suppose he would have been surprised that she had got work in a shop when she had that past conviction for robbery, but whether he knew she had actively lied, I don't know. And what would he care? I know what you're thinking," Cath said. "Was it a motive for killing Alec? It seems really too thin, because it is so long ago."

"You're right. Did anything else come up?"

"No, not really. She's single and has been since she came out of prison, or so she said. She mentioned she had an admirer but she has no idea who it might be. Someone has been delivering bouquets of daffodils to her."

"Daffodils aren't even in season."

"I know."

Penny said, "It wouldn't be Carl Fredericks, would it? He has a bulb business. Maybe he wants her back."

"We suggested that but her face was a picture. I doubt she'd take him back. We need to have another chat with Carl, though, now we have more of his lies exposed."

CHAPTER SIXTEEN

Wednesday night was exactly as awful as Penny expected it to be, and she was very grateful for Francine's patience and understanding. She moped around her cottage, looking at the abandoned dog toys which littered the floor, and tried not to get upset at the sight of the water bowl and empty basket.

Not that Kali often slept in her designated basket anyway. She was definitely a sofa-based animal.

She rang Drew and he was appalled and supportive. He was about to drop everything and come around, but she assured him that she was all right. Hearing his voice was enough of a comfort.

But she didn't tell him that.

She stared for a long hour at websites that listed everything that was poisonous to dogs that could be found around the house and in the garden, and then went outside to study her flower borders.

Nothing.

But thinking that it could have been a deliberate act was shocking and repellent.

She hardly slept at all.

* * * *

So Thursday was a groggy sort of day, both within Penny's self-fuddled head and reflected in the heavy grey weather outside. For the end of July, it was strangely cold and what Penny called "sweater weather". She pulled a thick jumper on and took comfort from its warmth.

Francine urged her to go for a walk. At first, Penny refused. Walks were for doing with dogs, and her dog was not there. But Francine was insistent that it would do her good. Eventually they wandered around the town centre, and then, by unspoken mutual accord, began to make their way south, in the direction of Alec Goodwin's house. The mystery of the unsolved murder drew them back, again and again.

"Are we going in?" Francine said as they stood at the gated entrance and looked down the driveway.

"I don't see the point," Penny said morosely. "I don't even know why we came down here."

"It calls to us," Francine said dramatically. "The universe wants us to do something. It needs closure."

Penny noted the use of "us" but ignored it. She couldn't ignore the "universe" though. "Do you actually believe that?"

"Why not? Prove me wrong. Something has caused us to walk down here."

"Yes. Feet."

Francine sniffed. "What propelled our feet, though? You can't deny that it calls to us. This house. This place. It calls to me, anyway."

"It's basic psychology, that's all," Penny said. "It's unfinished business and we are involved, so of course we will find ourselves here. It's just how minds work."

"There is a lot to do with our minds that hasn't been explained yet. Maybe science will have all the answers. But perhaps things that are considered a bit lunatic now will be eventually proved correct. What's that thing about sufficiently advanced technology being indistinguishable from magic?"

"You've got a point," Penny said. "Hmm. I wonder if Barry has spoken with Steve this past day or two."

She started forward, and Francine trailed along behind. "What about his dogs?"

"They are a pair of softies, you know that."

There was no need to worry. As they passed by Alec's house, and approached the shack where Barry lived, they saw that he was fixing the fence that was the boundary to his garden.

"Now then, Penny. Can't stay away from me, can you, ha ha!" He wiped his hands on his sweat-stained t-shirt and grinned. He nodded at Francine and winked.

He could get away with such cheekiness. Penny grinned back at him.

"Wasn't the fence Alec's responsibility?"

"Yeah, but I don't reckon he's going to have chance to do much about it now," Barry said. He was knocking u-shaped nails into wooden posts to hold the chicken-wire fence into place. Behind him, Bob and Cassandra tumbled together on the grass. "Anyway, I thought it was time I smartened it all up around here."

"What's going to happen to the house, and your place?"

"I dunno. It's all sort of stuck for the moment. It'll probably be sold. I'll carry on living here, quiet-like, until someone notices. Maybe the next owner will be a nice one."

"It is lovely out here," Francine said. "So peaceful. No neighbours and no noise. I love it."

Penny had to agree, and she nodded, but Barry was shaking his head. "Oh, you reckon? Most times, it is. Mind you, the last few weeks have been a bit hectic. Police everywhere, not to mention nosey-parkers like you two. At least you pair turn up in daylight, though."

"Why, have you have people poking around at night?" Penny asked.

"Yeah, last night some weirdo was sneaking around, yeah. The dogs went bananas so I let them out to chase them off."

Penny grimaced. Clearly Barry had little understanding of the trouble he'd be in if any would-be burglar decided to be terrified of the dogs. "Did the dogs catch the intruder? Have you told the police?"

"Nah, I ain't one for bothering the cops. Bob and

Cassandra sorted them right out. Whoever it was, they legged it. I don't know what they were up to, though. Look at the mess!" He turned and pointed his hammer in the direction of his residence.

"What is all that? Daffodils?" Penny said.

"Yeah. Daffodils in pots. Like they were setting them out around my front door. There was a gift tag on one of them. It even said 'to Barry' on it. Madness!"

"Wow. That is … strange."

Francine laughed. "You've got a secret admirer, obviously!"

Just like Mandy, Penny thought. *We've got to go and talk to Cath about this.*

"Good luck with the fence!" Penny said brightly. "Come on, Francine. Let's go…"

"Bye…"

Francine shot her a sideways glance but Penny pretended to not notice as she strode quickly back to the road, staying silent until they were well out of earshot.

As soon as she was certain that Barry couldn't hear them, she said to Francine, "We're going to Lincoln. Now."

240

* * * *

Francine drove in her little car, and Penny spent the first ten minutes dialling and redialling Cath until she finally answered.

"I was in the bathroom," was her opening statement.

"Too much information!"

"Sorry," said Cath. "No, wait. Not sorry. Is this a matter of life and death?"

"Yes. Alec's death."

Cath was suddenly serious. "Go on."

"We're on our way up to Lincoln. Can we meet?"

"Come into the station," Cath said. "I'll find us a room. Who is 'we' – is Drew with you?"

"No, Francine."

"Okay. See you soon. Drive carefully. Hang on! You don't have a hands-free."

"Francine's driving."

Cath growled and hung up.

Then Penny called the veterinary surgery to get an update on Kali. She got through more quickly than she had to Cath, and was reassured that Kali was up on her feet, a little groggy, but would be okay to collect and take home in two hours' time.

"Thank goodness," Francine said as Penny relayed the news.

When they reached the police station, Cath was waiting. The desk sergeant grimaced when he saw Penny and Francine.

"Oh, no. There's more of them."

Cath waved at him and ushered them both into a sparse, beige interview room. "I've got information," she said as they sat on unpleasant plastic chairs around the table, "but go on. I'd like to hear yours, first."

"Daffodils," Penny said. "There is something really strange going on with daffodils right now, and that points to Carl Fredericks, or … I hate to say it, but to Ginni Llewellyn."

"Just because Mandy Jones had daffodils delivered to her?"

"And so has Barry Neville."

"Crikey," Cath said. "Barry has an admirer, does he?"

"What sort of admirer creeps around someone's house in the middle of the night and puts out a few pots of

242

daffodils?" Penny said. "And most weird of all … daffodils aren't even in season."

"That's true," Cath said. "How did you find this out?"

Penny and Francine's words fell over each other as they took turns in explaining what had happened. Cath pulled out a notebook and jotted a few things down. "And do you believe Barry?" she asked. "Or is it something he's done to throw us all off the scent?"

"It's a strange way to do it. He wouldn't have known that Mandy had been given flowers, would he?"

"Unless he sent them."

"Do Barry and Mandy know one another?"

Cath shook her head. "They don't seem to, and we haven't found any links."

"Mandy has admitted staying in touch with Carl, and we know that Carl had more knowledge of Alec's current lifestyle than he admits to," Penny said. "Did Mandy ever visit Alec's house? She could have met Barry."

Cath smiled. "Well, that brings you on to my information. We've examined all the mobile phone and landline logs for all these suspects. Alec called Mandy at nine on Saturday morning. Yes, the Saturday that he was killed."

"So he had got her number from Carl?" Penny said.

"Yes. Therefore it confirms that Carl and Mandy were still in touch, just as she said. And it also shows that Alec and Mandy had, indeed, lost touch."

"And Carl and Alec…?" Penny said, trying to get the triangle laid out in her head.

"We think they must have had some contact, at least recently," Cath said. "However, Carl is denying it and we can't ask Alec."

Penny rubbed her face and sighed. "Right. So, Alec called Mandy. She denied it, didn't she?"

"We put that information to her when we called her in, and faced with the evidence, she admitted that he had called her. And she said she'd been surprised. But then, there's more. They met up on Saturday afternoon."

"Oh my goodness! Alec and Mandy met? Where? She could have poisoned him, then."

Cath nodded. "She's shot right up the suspect list, yes. Not least for all her lies and omissions. They met in a public beer garden of a quiet country pub that afternoon, and talked."

"What about?"

"She was still being evasive. It's like prying a winkle out of a shell. She said that she forgave him. We pressed her on that, and she finally told us about her stint in prison."

"Ah!" Penny said. "So, was her sentence something to do with Alec?"

"Yes," Cath said. "In fact, Alec's evidence was crucial in convicting her."

All three were silent while the implications of that revelation sunk in.

"Hang on," Francine said after a short while. She ticked things off on her fingers as she spoke. "Let me get this straight. Mandy was part of a gang that robbed a jewellery shop twenty years ago. Mandy was married to Carl. Carl and Alec were best friends. And then Alec gave evidence which convicted Mandy for her part in the robbery."

Cath nodded.

"I'm not as bright as you two," Francine said. "How on earth did Alec have any evidence that Mandy was involved?"

"Because he was a court artist with a photographic memory," Cath explained. "And he was sitting in the trial for the jewellery heist, and when they described the female accomplice, he realised it was Mandy."

"Oh." Penny sat back. "That must have been so painful for both Alec and Carl. He couldn't keep quiet, could he, Alec? And yet doing the right thing would destroy his friend and his friend's marriage. Wow."

"Poor Alec, and poor Carl," Francine added.

"It's a bad business, all round," said Cath. "Of course, it could all be co-incidence that Mandy met Alec that day."

"She has reason to have a massive grudge against him!" Penny said. "My goodness. If I had done ten years in prison because of my ex-husband's best mate, I'd be very annoyed."

"Ahh," said Cath, wagging her finger. "She didn't do ten years because of Alec. She did ten years because she committed a crime."

Penny blew out her cheeks. "True, true. And she seemed to harbour no malice when we met her."

"To be honest," Cath said, "she gives the impression of being at peace with her past, now. She's done her time and paid her debt to society and now all she wants to do is to live quietly."

"But she can't, can she?" Penny said. "Because she lied on her job application and Alec must have known!"

"Again, we can't be certain…"

"It's a pretty good assumption."

"We do not convict on assumptions," Cath said warningly.

"She was a criminal," Penny said. She could almost feel herself pouting.

"*Was*," Cath said.

Francine butted in. "People can change, Penny. In fact, people must change. I believe that utterly. Otherwise, what's the point? If we can't try to be a little bit better every day that we wake up, we might as well give up."

"You're one sentence away from saying that the universe responds to goodness, aren't you?"

"You took the words right out of my mouth," Francine said happily.

Penny narrowed her eyes and stared at Francine, searching for a hint of sarcasm. There was none. She turned back to Cath. "Any more revelations?"

"No, sorry. But I thought you'd like to know this."

"Yes. Thanks."

"Are you all right?"

"Oh, Kali, and I'm tired, and … everything."

"Of course, I'm so sorry. How is she?" Cath asked.

"We're on our way to collect her. She is going to be okay," Penny said. "But I won't be letting her out of my sight again."

"Off you go."

Within an hour, they had collected the weak but happy dog, and were back on their way to Upper Glenfield.

CHAPTER SEVENTEEN

By the next morning, Kali was bouncing around as if nothing had ever happened. Penny and Francine spent the morning in the garden, talking over and over and over about the murder case.

Penny felt as if she were no nearer an answer, and it was making her grumpy. The worry about Kali, and Francine's constant apologising didn't help, either. Finally Francine excused herself in the early afternoon, and disappeared on a walk, leaving Penny and Kali alone. Penny tried to do some craft work. She had the stencilled fabric to make up into bags, but Kali was keen to go out again, and Penny felt so bad about the dog's recent experiences that she was inclined to put her work down and take some more time out.

So when Drew rang her, around four in the afternoon,

and offered her "an unusual culinary experience in a unique setting, and you can bring the dog," she jumped at the distraction.

She sent a text to Francine. Drew had advised her to "dress warmly; I'll collect you in an hour's time." She knew instantly what he had in mind for her, but she resolved to act surprised anyway. It was only polite.

But he guessed.

"You know, don't you?" he said. They had parked in a quiet lane and walked up along a bridleway that became a footpath, following the edge of a small piece of woodland. He was carrying a small knapsack.

"Know what?"

"That I'm treating you to a meal out. Literally, a meal outside."

"You gave it away when you told me to dress warmly and bring Kali."

"I suppose I did. But hopefully I have some surprises left for you tonight."

She felt a warm flutter in her stomach, but quashed it. Drew had only ever been a friend to her. A good friend, yes, but a friend. He had once made a slightly blue remark, totally off the cuff, and had immediately apologised and taken it back. Penny wasn't sure if it had been indicative of some deeper feelings in him, or he had simply spoken without thinking.

As he had never given her any further signs that he might want to take the relationship to a new level, she had to concede that he was simply a platonic friend.

She was sad about that. When their friendship had begun, she'd seen it as the start of a potential courtship. It had felt like that "getting to know you" phase between a new couple. But it had never gone beyond that.

They were "just friends."

Was it because he was so busy? It was an argument she'd used in her head, excusing him, for a long time. Now she had to put that aside.

They really *were* "just friends."

And he was a good friend, so she was going to enjoy this friendship, and not spoil it for wanting it to be something that it was not.

"You're lost in thought," Drew said.

"I'm sorry? What were you saying?" Penny was embarrassed to have been caught out. Drew and Kali were both standing still and staring at her.

"That this is a good spot for us."

There was a small, grassy area, bordered by the trees, and then a hedge in front of them and the fields beyond. It was like a hidden half-moon lawn between the woods and the agriculture, the grass close-cropped by rabbits. Drew dropped his knapsack and Penny walked around the perimeter of the small area, letting Kali sniff all the details that they could not see.

When she turned back around, Drew was on his knees, digging a hole.

"Are you doing what I think you're doing?" she asked, horrified.

He sat back, the small trowel wedged upright in the soil. "I'm digging a fire pit."

"Oh!"

He laughed uproariously. "You thought I was digging some kind of wilderness latrine, didn't you?"

"No," she said. "Okay, yes."

He pointed at the trees. "Go in there if you need to. I can lend you my trowel."

"Um. Thanks."

Drew carefully peeled back the grassy sods and laid them to one side. Then he got up and went in search of twigs and sticks, assisted by Kali, while Penny set about unpacking the knapsack.

Once the fire was lit, he unfolded a small iron tripod that he had clearly made himself. "Can you pass me that small box?" he asked, pointing at a plastic container with a clip-top lid.

"What's in it?"

He flipped it open and showed her. There were a few eggs, nestling around a knobbly black lump with warty bits. "Dinner."

"I can't eat … coal? No, what is it?"

"It's a summer truffle. You get them more to the south, and in Europe, but I stumbled on this yesterday – actually there were a few but I left the rest. I'm going to do scrambled eggs. Honestly, it will be lovely."

"I've had truffles but they weren't quite like that."

"You probably had the more common Burgundy truffles. This isn't as strong. You'll like it!"

"Okay." Penny grinned in delight. "I love trying new food. It was one of the best bits about all the travelling I used to do. Some members of the production team would only ever eat stuff they knew about, like fish and chips, but what's the point of that?"

"Do you know what hairy bittercress looks like?" Drew asked.

"Nope. Why, do you want me to go and find some?"

"I think I'd better come and show you," he said. "Just in case."

Soon they were sitting on a spread rug, and the wonderful smell of outdoor cooking was mingling with the wood smoke.

"This reminds me of being a kid," Penny said, as Drew prodded the scrambling eggs, enriched by the truffles and the small green leaves of bittercress.

"Is it just the one sister that you've got?" he asked innocently. "Ariadne, that's right, isn't it?"

"Yeah." She thought she'd told Drew that she did not get on with Ariadne. She assumed her flat tone would give him the hint that she didn't want to talk about her. She'd managed to push her out of her mind since the unexpected phone call.

"And your parents, they travel a lot, don't they?"

"Yeah," she said, brightening up. "They are all over the place. I never know where they are until I get a postcard, and by then, they are usually somewhere else."

"That's great. Um, you don't see much of Ariadne, do you? Oh, pass us that plate. Brilliant. Here you go, eggs and truffle."

"Thank you!" She ate with gusto and it was fantastic. But she knew she was avoiding his question, and she had to answer. "Well, I spoke to Ariadne on the phone, actually. She rang me, out of the blue."

"Oh. Is everything all right?"

"I suppose so."

"Suppose?"

Penny sighed deeply. "I don't know. I doubt it. I just don't understand why she doesn't leave that oaf, you know? Her husband, Owen, he creeps me out."

"How?"

"There's something about him that I didn't like, right from the start."

"Well," Drew said, "if they are in love, though, it makes it all okay."

"No, he spoke to her in a funny way. Not in a

respectful way. I'm not old fashioned but … there was something off about him. And the stupid thing is, I wouldn't say he was abusive, but he seemed to make her into a different person, just through words, and I didn't like it."

"Have they got kids?"

"Yes," Penny said. "With stupid hippy names. Star, Destiny and Wolf. How cruel."

"I don't know," Drew said. "I quite like them. 'Destiny' is hardly unheard of. They are individual. And it's common to have uncommon names these days, so I doubt they'd get teased. One of the lads at the school I'm working at, he's called Prince."

"No way!"

"Seriously. Prince. But although it seemed odd at first, it soon becomes just a name, you know? Anyway, so you're an aunt!"

"Hmm." Penny felt a pang of guilt, and it took her by surprise. She had lost touch with her nieces and nephew just as much as she had with Ariadne and Owen. "I suppose that I am. I don't take my duties seriously, though."

Drew wisely refrained from comment. He poured

some sparkling drink. "Here, try this. It's elderflower."

She sniffed and it prickled her nose. "Oh! It smells much better than elderflowers do."

"Oh, did you make the mistake of picking them and bringing them inside?"

"Yes," she said. "I thought they'd make a nice floral display. But everything smelled of tom cat wee."

"They are said to be bad luck inside a house," Drew said.

"I am not surprised."

They fell silent for a moment. Penny didn't want to talk about Ariadne. But now she was thinking about her more and more, and realising that some of her past actions were not, exactly, stellar.

In fact, she may have behaved in a very unpleasant way.

Which led her to a choice. Continue, or change?

Change was hard.

Drew must have been watching her internal dialogue. He pulled the knapsack over and said, "Time for pudding, then!"

"Oh, more cheating. We're not foraging for it."

"The truffles weren't really cheating. They *were* foraged.

But if you could tell me in which region I can find naturally-growing battenburg cake, I'd be very impressed."

She laughed and the tension was broken.

As they packed up to go home, Drew remarked, casually, "So have you heard the news about Steve, then?"

"Ginni's nephew? The Sculpture Trail guy?"

"That's exactly it," Drew said. "He's not the Sculpture Trail guy any longer."

"Who is?"

"I don't know, and I wondered if you did."

"I didn't even know about Steve," she said. "Was it because of his meltdown the other night?"

"I heard he flipped out in public, yeah."

"I wonder what he's going to do now," she mused as they walked back towards Drew's car.

"I wonder what's going to happen to the trail," Drew said.

CHAPTER EIGHTEEN

Penny and Francine walked with Kali through the town centre. Francine wanted to visit the market, and Penny was just pleased to be out and about. The evening with Drew had been fun, and although Francine pressed her for gory details that simply didn't exist, Penny found she was content with things as they stood – at least for the moment.

Penny waited outside the covered market hall with Kali while Francine dived inside to look at the fish stall. She'd only been gone three minutes when she came running out again, her hands empty.

"The Sculpture Trail's been sabotaged!" she gasped out. "I just heard!"

Penny was surprised. "But the Sculpture Trail doesn't even exist yet," she said. "You can't sabotage an invisible walking trail."

"The wooden poles, and the things that Steve had started to do before he stopped, was all being kept in a back room at the Community Hall," Francine told her. "Come on. Let's go."

"Where?"

"The hall!"

Francine strode off, and Kali followed, leaving Penny to be hauled along in their wake. And they were not the only ones making their way there. Mary was there, and Agatha, and Reg, and a few others that had nothing better to do with their day.

And also there was Ginni, who must have left her shop in the charge of someone else. *Possibly Steve*, Penny thought.

Francine had no qualms about forcing her way into the hall with everyone else. Penny dithered for a moment, wondering whether it was all right to bring Kali in. Francine beckoned at them frantically, and Penny rolled her eyes and followed.

Kali wanted to sniff all the new smells in the hall but Penny clicked her tongue and got her to walk nicely to the back, where everyone was gathered around an open doorway.

Penny peeked in.

It was a scene of devastation. The store room ran the length of the back of the hall, and it looked as if a hurricane had blown through. Wood was scattered around, and she assumed those were the remains of the poles for the trail, now broken and shattered. Large sheets of paper with scribbled drawings on were ripped up and torn. There was smashed clay in lumps and finished fired pottery shards on the floor.

Penny stayed in the hall, peeking in. People chattered in shock and horror, but with an undercurrent of excitement. It was natural human curiosity, but still it left a bad taste in Penny's mouth.

Francine had pushed forward into the store room, and was gazing around, her usually narrow eyes wide in shock. "Who could have done this? Oh, poor Steve."

"He was off the Sculpture Trail anyway," Penny said in a low voice, aware of the proximity of Ginni. *And maybe that was why … he could have done this out of spite.*

Ginni heard her speak. She walked past Penny and joined Francine in the back room.

"I'm so sorry," Francine said. "It looks like it's all over."

Ginni looked around, and straightened her back as she lifted her head. "No. It simply means we begin again."

"How? This will be the third attempt. It won't be done for this August's fair, will it, eh?" Agatha said, who was standing just behind Penny, and peering around her arm into the store room. "Maybe it's a sign. Maybe it's best to stop trying to hurry it forward, and look at it for next year."

"How long until the fair?" Francine asked. "A week?"

"A week," said Ginni, her firm jaw raised and set. Penny wished she had a camera. Ginni wouldn't have looked out of place as a stone statue in revolutionary Russia.

Francine was as transfixed by Ginni as Penny was. "One week," she echoed. "Right. So, is any of this salvageable?"

Agatha nudged Penny with her elbow. "What are they doing?"

"It looks like they are sorting out the wooden poles," Penny said.

"I know that, eh, but what are they *doing?*"

Penny sighed. "Something impossible."

Francine and Ginni had rolled up their sleeves and were sorting through the chaos and the rubbish. Penny watched them for a moment, then said, "You can't do this on your own."

She meant that she was prepared to help out, even though it seemed doomed to failure. But Ginni stopped and threw up her head.

"Yes. Yes! You're right!" She swallowed and pinked slightly. "I might have to concede that in some respects, ahem, I could have acted hastily and somewhat foolishly in the past. However, it may never be said that I am too stubborn…"

Agatha coughed and choked but Ginni ignored her.

"And I feel," Ginni continued, "that if I might be allowed to eat a little humble pie, then perhaps we can, indeed, galvanise the whole town into action. You're perfectly correct, Penelope. We cannot do this on our own. But with the community behind us … why yes, we might move mountains!"

"How … what?" Penny said. "I mean, that sounds great in practise, but you will need longer than a week."

Ginni turned and met her eyes, and Penny tried not to step back, such was the force of the woman's glare. "We are *women*," she said firmly. "We get things done."

Ginni turned back to Francine. "Right. We shall tidy up, and list what remains useable. Then we will retreat to the local pub and create an action plan. Paper and pen?"

Francine had already grabbed a sheet of paper from the carnage on the floor. "Let's do it."

Penny backed into the hall, away from the feverish energy that was crackling in the store room between the two surprising and formidable women. Agatha and the others remained, and most were silent as they listened to the plans tumbling around from Ginni and Francine.

Well, Penny thought. *Francine had been a great television producer. She might just pull this off. Her lateral thinking and problem solving, married to Ginni's bulldozer personality … yes, of all the people in this crazy town, they are the ones to sort the Sculpture Trail out, indeed.*

* * * *

She was only a few yards from the community hall when Drew pulled up in his car. Kali bounded up and put her paws on the open window, shoving her head into the car to greet him.

264

"I am so sorry! Kali, down, you great lump."

The dog thumped back to the ground, unrepentantly wagging her tail.

"Is it true?" Drew asked, sticking his hand out of the window to scratch Kali's head.

"That the art for the trail has been trashed? Yes, it is. I don't know who, though I have my suspicions. But something even stranger is happening in there. Ginni and Francine are having *ideas*."

"Oh. Oh, er, right. I'll not go in," he said.

"Best not."

"Anyway. I was on my way to see you."

"This way?" she said.

"Okay, so I was on a detour to check this news out first."

"I'm shocked at you, Drew," she said, laughing. "You say you're not interested in gossip!"

"Being with you has obviously affected me," he said darkly.

She bit back her flirty retort, and instead she said, "I can't imagine anyone making you do something you didn't want to do."

"Huh. Anyway … I thought you'd want to hear this. And it's sort of gossip, except it isn't, it's news. I mean, it's gossip if I heard about it from someone else, but news if it's happened to me, right?"

"I think that's how it goes," said Penny. "So what is your news-not-gossip?"

"Barry came to see me."

Penny gaped at him. "He did? Why?"

Drew was still absently stroking Kali. "I'm not totally sure. I mean, everyone around here knows one another, and everyone certainly knows me and they know I'm doing work at that school. Barry said it was because of that, because I'm down to earth and don't have any 'side' as he calls it."

"But what did he say?" Penny implored, half-expecting a full confession to murder.

"He said that Steve was avoiding everyone and everything, and that he was in a bad way. And he also said that he knew that him and Steve were each other's alibis and that it looked dodgy and he didn't want to seem to be colluding with him."

"Colluding?"

"Okay, so Barry didn't use those exact words, but that's what he meant. And the thing he wanted, was that he wanted to go and speak to Steve and try to help him, but he didn't want to do it on his own, because of all that."

Penny frowned. "Let me get this straight. Steve is all upset, and Barry wants to talk to him, but he wants your help to talk to him?"

"Yes, exactly."

"Wow. That's interesting."

"He seemed really embarrassed, did Barry. He apologised for not being very 'manly' and I laughed at him for that, but he meant it. He thought he was being 'soft' for wanting to help his friend but he knew it was what he had to do."

"Are they really friends?"

"They are. I think they just enjoy how easy it is to be in one another's space."

"The simplicity of their company," Penny mused, suddenly struck by the notion.

"Yeah, if you say so."

"Have you been to see Steve, then?"

"No," said Drew. "Not yet. We're going to seek him

out tonight, with the help of a few cans of beer and maybe a bag of peanuts."

"The tempting lure of peanuts."

"Do you think Steve was anything to do with what's going on in there? Could he have trashed the Sculpture Trail?"

She nodded sadly. "I think so. Perhaps you can find out tonight. Good luck."

Drew waved and began to put the car into gear. "Thanks. I'll let you know how it goes."

"Please do. Oh, and Drew – I think it's a really nice thing that you're doing, you know."

He laughed it off. "Just being neighbourly."

She watched him drive away. Kali was sitting down, and looking up at her with a bored expression. She'd sniffed everything within range, and was patiently waiting to move on.

Penny was thoughtful. Drew really did believe Barry and what he had said. Drew took people at face value.

Penny was not so sure.

CHAPTER NINETEEN

Penny didn't hear from Drew that night, and she assumed he was still with Barry on his mission to help Steve. She sent a text message to him the following day, but there was no reply until the evening.

"Went well."

That was it? She glared at the screen. *You infuriating man. What about Steve? What about Barry? What was that man hiding?*

She had spent the day completely absorbed – as much as she could be – in her arts and crafts work, and Francine had been conspicuously absent until she barged into the cottage at half past five, clutching two bags of hot chips wrapped in paper, and saying,

"You've got to come to the meeting!"

"What meeting?"

"The Sculpture Trail Extraordinary Meeting. It's in the hall, in half an hour. Come on. Let's eat and go. Battered sausage all right for you?"

"Do I have a choice?"

Francine swept through into the kitchen, followed by Kali who was sure there must be something wrapped up for her, too. "No."

* * * *

The Community Hall was much fuller than Penny had expected. "How did everyone find out?"

"The town grapevine," Francine said. "Well, me and Ginni going round everyone's houses and shops and everything. Obviously a lot of people are still at work or commuting home, but this is a pretty good turnout."

"It is."

Lots of people had brought their children, probably because they couldn't get childcare with such late notice, and the hall was noisy with chattering and laughter. Francine stood on tip-toes to look over the heads of the crowd towards the top table.

"Ah! Ginni's there. I've got to go," she said to Penny, and disappeared into the throng.

"Right." Penny sighed and waited.

Soon the meeting was called to order, and people took their seats. It was just over half-full, Penny reckoned. Ginni and Francine stood side by side in front of the table, and both were smiling.

Francine was still Francine. She was still the laughing, giggling, warm and exuberant person that Penny was so familiar with. She still used phrases like "the love that this town has for the project is what will make it a success!" and "this belongs to *you*, Upper Glenfield!" but coming from Francine, they sounded fine. Penny couldn't say things like that without sounding like a politician with a hidden agenda. But Francine had no agenda. Her openness had been her key to success in the corporate world.

Or had it? Penny thought back to Francine's reasons to leaving London. Penny had always known that some people laughed at Francine. To her shame, she herself had smiled along, sometimes, when she'd wanted to ingratiate herself into a group.

Francine's talents had been so wasted, Penny realised

as she gazed up at the passionate woman on the platform. She had a truth in her energy that these people responded to. They *wanted* to believe her.

So they did.

And Ginni was the seal of approval that the town's residents also needed. With Ginni beside her, Francine wasn't an incomer to be suspicious of. She was accepted; Ginni's proximity saw to that.

"All of us!" Francine was saying. "We are all together in this! Ginni, perhaps you can explain what has already been achieved just this very day!"

Ginni stepped forward. Her manner was drier and more straightforward, but the content of her speech far outweighed her factual delivery.

Penny was amazed.

The local care home for the elderly had begun already, with some of their willing residents working with one of the occupational health staff who happened to have an interest in pottery. They were collaborating on a design of a barn owl, as there were regularly seen in the area.

The scouts, guides and beaver groups had been contacted, and the leaders were keen to get everyone involved. They were going to produce a clay figure each.

The vicar from the church in the centre of town was keen. He'd been tracked down at one of his satellite churches a few miles away – he never seemed to be in the same place for more than two hours – but he had a full programme of house groups he was going to galvanise into action.

Even the market traders' association that represented the stallholders in the covered market had welcomed the ideas and were planning a clay model of their own.

When Ginni had finished, there was rapturous applause for a minute.

It was too good to last.

A man shouted out, "Yeah, but, yeah, the clay, right, the clay is still going to break in the frost, isn't it?"

All eyes stared at Ginni and Francine.

Penny shook her head. People could be so infuriating. Steve had been right; she knew that properly prepared and sealed stoneware would be weather-proof. But Steve's ideas had not been viewed with confidence, and it was a stumbling block to the whole project.

"There is another way."

The voice came from the back of the hall. A low rumble of chatter started up as three men entered and walked up the central aisle to the platform at the top.

Steve had spoken, and he was flanked by Barry and Drew. When they reached the platform, the whole hall held its breath.

Francine smiled widely. "Steve! Come on up. Tell us about your way."

Everyone exhaled. Steve shook his head, and hunched his shoulders, unwilling to step up into the limelight again. But he spoke loud enough for everyone to hear.

"So what we wanna do, you see, is use the clay models as moulds. You should encourage everyone to make tiles, not round objects. You know, like what I was gonna do and all that. We press the designs into casting sand and pour molten aluminium into the impression. There you go, metal designs to screw onto poles. We were looking at the maps and stuff, and we reckon we won't even need that many new poles. There's a lot of places we can put them already, you know, fences and that."

Someone snorted with laughter. "How are going to melt aluminium? In a saucepan?"

Drew stepped up onto the platform, and spread his hands wide as he faced the crowd. "Um, do you know anyone with a furnace?"

People began to look at one another and laugh and nod. Drew folded his arms and grinned. Penny could see that a part of him was lapping up the limelight and she grinned, hoping to catch his eye.

He saw her, and she was sure that he winked.

Maybe.

Francine, Drew, Ginni and Steve were the centre of everyone's attention.

Penny faded into the background, and told herself that she was very, very happy for them all.

* * * *

Penny was sitting in the living room with Kali curled up next to her on the sofa. She had one lamp lit, and was listening to music.

Finally she heard the front door open and close, and the stealthy entrance of Francine walking like someone who was trying not to disturb anyone. She jumped as she came into the living room, her shoes in her hand.

"Oh! Sorry, I thought you'd be in bed."

"I feel like a mother waiting for her teenage daughter to come home," Penny said.

"I was talking, and I got carried away. Sorry, again. I should have sent a text."

"Don't apologise," Penny said, laughing. "You've nothing to apologise for. I am not your mother…"

"Thank goodness," Francine said, dropping her shoes.

Penny had never asked about Francine's family. "Are you not close?"

She shuddered. "No, not at all. I was never good enough or hard enough or dedicated enough."

"You're kidding!" Penny sat up and stared at Francine in the half-light. "You were an amazing and highly successful career woman."

"Ah, well, mum was a politician *and* a professor of economics."

"Really? Wow."

"Yeah," said Francine, "and of course I'm very proud of her. Well, one of us has to be."

"She must be proud of you. It's a mother thing, isn't it?"

Francine sighed heavily and when she spoke, her voice was low. "A mother thing? I don't think there *is* a mother thing. Or my mother was at the back of the queue, or busy with something dreadfully dreadfully important … more important than family. We're all different."

Penny briefly closed her eyes. "Yes, that's true." She forced a change of subject, for both their sakes. "Right. So, that meeting. You were fantastic! You know, I think you two might just pull it off."

"Us two? No, it's the whole town," Francine said, beaming once more, her rubber-ball nature refusing to stay quashed.

"Well done us, then."

* * * *

Penny slept badly and remembered the old Spanish proverb about not blaming one's bed: *first examine your conscience.* As soon as the shops were open, she headed out to the florist's shop along the High Street.

Ginni was behind the counter, looking fresh and full of life. She was clearly pleased to be part of things again.

"Can I order flowers to be delivered through you, but quite far away? Are you part of that network?" Penny asked.

"Of course. Whereabouts?"

"Leicestershire." Penny pulled out her address book and read out the directions. "It's for my sister."

If Ginni thought it odd that Penny didn't know her own sister's address very well, she was too polite to say. *She must have to exercise quite a degree of discretion*, Penny thought. *All those people having affairs, and secret admirers, and people saying sorry for this and for that.*

"Sorry" was sort of what Penny was saying to Ariadne. "Something cheerful," she said when Ginni asked what she wanted. "It's not an occasion like a birthday. It's just a way of saying hello, and that I hope everything is all right."

"Right. Summery and happy, a riot of colours." Ginni pointed at various pre-made displays. "Like that one?"

"Just like that. Thank you." Penny gazed around. It seemed quite cold in the shop, in contrast to the warmth outside. "This place is amazing. I've not been in before."

Ginni smiled. "I worked hard for this shop. I nearly lost it after my divorce but my friends helped me and it worked out in the end. It's everything to me, now. Would you like to see in the back?"

"Oh, yes please!"

Penny was keen to see new things, but there was an ulterior motive that she hardly even admitted to herself. Ginni, or at least Ginni and Steve, were still on her list of suspects for the murder of Alec Goodwin. And she had been puzzling about the daffodils that had been sent to Mandy, and delivered in the night to Barry.

And so it was daffodils that she was particularly interested in as she nosed around the very cold stock room.

"It's like an ice box in here!" she said. "There must be a reason for it."

"I'm tight with money. Oh, and it is better for the plants," Ginni said. "You do get used to it. Steve still grumbles, but that's just him."

"He did a big thing, coming back to the public meeting."

"Yes, he did, and I am glad," Ginni said. "I guess me and him are alike. Stubborn, but we come around in the end."

"What about the fact that he didn't graduate?" Penny said. "What is he going to do?"

"I'll admit that I was shocked," Ginni said, idly sorting

out some long-stemmed plants, arranging them in a wooden bucket. "But we talked, and then we went to my sister's house – his mum, you know – and we all talked, and maybe there was some alcohol consumed, and when we all woke up the next day, things did not seem quite so bad. What hurt us all the most were his lies."

"He was worried."

"Yes," Ginni said. "And actually, it wasn't the lies so much as the fact that he felt he *had* to lie to us. Anyway, it's all water under the bridge, as they say. I know he has his issues, and he gets a little too angry, but I am sure he'll grow up soon."

Penny made a non-committal noise and browsed along the workbench to where some bulbs were laid out in trays. She picked one up and looked at it. "Now, is this a tuber or a corm?" she asked, trying to sound like she knew what she was talking about.

"Neither," said Ginni. "It's a true bulb."

"Daffodil?"

"Yes, so you have better wash your hands before you eat anything. Did you know there was a spate of people eating daffodil bulbs because they thought they were some strange Chinese vegetable?"

"Will it kill you?" Penny said.

"Oh no, not at all, but you'd be ill."

"Oh." She put it down on the tray again. "Well, I'll let you get on. Thank you for sorting out the bunch of flowers for me…"

"My pleasure."

* * * *

Penny's head was whirling and she phoned Cath as soon as she had got away from the shop. She walked over the road and headed to the peace and quiet of the churchyard, settling on a bench under a broad, spreading yew.

She glanced around but there was no one else by the graves. She didn't want to disturb anyone's peace, but as she found herself alone, she thought it was probably all right.

Cath didn't pick up her mobile. Penny hunted in her purse for the small business card that Cath had given her, all those months ago when they had first met at the death of the farmer, David Hart. It had Cath's alternate numbers listed, and Penny tried her office phone.

A man answered. "Inspector Travis. How can I help?"

"Oh! Hi, it's Penny May. Is DC Pritchard around, please?"

"She's out and about. Hi, Penny. How is it going?"

"Slowly. I'm really sorry. I think I'm letting you all down."

"Not at all, not at all. I think the conversations you've had with Cath have been quite useful."

Penny felt funny but of course Cath would have reported everything back to her Inspector. It was her job, after all. "Really? Have you made any progress that you can tell me about?"

"I can, as it happens. Toxicology reports are finally in. We know exactly what killed Alec Goodwin now."

"Oh!"

"Yes," the Inspector said. "Poet's narcissus."

"Er – what?"

"It's a type of plant, apparently. We're investigating further."

"Thank you for letting me know."

Penny let her phone drop into her lap and she stared around the green and leafy churchyard. Some bees were buzzing nearby. It was calm and peaceful.

But her mind was humming more frantically than even the bees. A plant had killed Alec Goodwin.

Ginni. Steve. Carl. Mandy.

It had to be one of them.

Or some of them, working together.

Didn't it?

CHAPTER TWENTY

When Penny got back to the cottage, she was surprised to find Francine there. Francine explained that she was taking a break, and making lists of things to do. Later on she was planning to meet Ginni, leaving Steve in charge at the florist's shop.

When Penny mentioned the new development in the Alec Goodwin case, Francine beset her with questions that she could not answer. They resorted to the internet and discovered that poet's narcissus was, indeed, a type of daffodil – but that the bulb was far more poisonous than the usual kind.

Poison, poison, poison. Penny sat in the kitchen while Francine made a cup of tea, and Kali skittered around, pushing her nose into the corners and huffing in search of stray crumbs.

"Kali seems to be recovering well," Penny said.

"Yes. I wonder what it was that made her ill?"

"So do I," Penny said, *thinking, poison, poison, poison.*

The fear gnawed at her bones, making her feel tired and heavy. She was prepared to risk many things in the pursuit of truth, but not her dog's own life.

"Don't worry," Francine urged, plonking the mug of tea down on the table in front of Penny. "Would you like me to take her for a walk, and let you relax? You look like you need it."

"Thank you. You have been so helpful. I don't want to impose on your good nature."

"It's no trouble!" Francine exclaimed. She knelt down on the hard floor and opened her arms to Kali who trotted over in expectation of food, or fuss, or both.

The scene was a long way from how they'd first met, with Kali leaping out of the door to knock Francine over, the first time Francine had come to visit.

"We love spending time together, don't we, snuggles?" Francine said, sniffing the top of Kali's head. Then she stood up somewhat awkwardly. "But she does love her mummy more."

"I am not her mummy," Penny said stiffly. "That's just weird."

Francine looked at Kali and winked, but wisely did not pursue it. "Seriously, it's fine. We have fun together. It's good for me, I think. So you're not imposing, all right?"

"I'm sorry. Okay, thank you for the offer, but I think I'm going to take some time out to clear my head. You know, I'm going to do something mad and spontaneous. Me and Kali, we're going to go camping."

Francine simply smiled brightly. "That sounds like a wonderful idea!"

* * * *

Four hours later, in the late afternoon, and Penny was starting to regret her decision, even though she'd only been walking for an hour. She had an old rucksack and a sleeping bag, and she had managed to track Drew down to borrow a tent from him, complete with hasty instructions on how to put it up. He seemed amused but unsurprised by her sudden need to get away from it all.

The rucksack's straps dug into her shoulders, the

weight pulling on her upper bag. The waist band of the rucksack was broken and now Penny was having flashbacks to her time in Girl Guides. Kali was oblivious to Penny's troubles and was scampering from side to side, delighted to be out on an adventure.

Penny plunged on, letting her feet do the thinking for her. She recited all the clues and suspects in her head.

A type of daffodil killed Alec. This was a fact and she kept returning to it. But there were other clues. What had she missed? She'd been there from the start, after all. Right from when Steve had run into the community hall.

She recalled what he'd said.

A van. A van that might have been white, or might have been red, or more likely it was a van that was dirty.

But dirty with something red?

Not blood. Think, Penny, think.

Dust. The red Saharan dust that blew over the fens in the summer. Yes. So it was a local van.

Ginni's van was spotless. Steve saw to that. Or was that a cover-up? She groaned and Kali looked up at her in surprise.

What else, she thought, pleading with her brain to make

sense of it all.

The path she was following led into some woods. She'd looked at a map and suggested her proposed itinerary to Drew, who had advised her to make for this remoter spot. This small woodland didn't have a car park and was so less likely to have other walkers around. Even so, he had suggested she did not pitch her tent until it was dusk.

He had also lent her his trowel, and winked.

She came into a pleasant clearing. It was no use. She had to drop her pack and massage her aching shoulders and neck. Kali was wearing a new harness, and Penny had tied a metal spike with a spiral base to the side of her pack. She drove it into the ground and tethered Kali on a long line, something she had not been able to do when Kali was wearing a head collar.

She poured a bowl of water and popped it into the shade of a bush, and then let Kali explore the limits of her tethered freedom. Penny sat in a sunny spot, perched on her pack, and rested her elbows on her bare knees.

What else?

Mandy, ex-criminal Mandy. The woman floated in her mind's eye, but all mixed up. Penny's first sight of her had been as she was, twenty years ago. The court case, the photographs, the artwork in Alec's studio.

Mandy was the link. Maybe she was the murderer, but really? Just so that she could keep her job as a sales assistant?

Penny's eyes were half closed as she looked into the past, and she wasn't watching Kali. All of a sudden, she was knocked off her makeshift seat as Kali erupted into a torrent of angry, snarling barking. The dog was foaming at the mouth as she leaped past Penny, and the long line caught Penny in the middle of the back, pitching her forwards onto her knees.

"Kali! *Down!*" she yelled. Giving a positive instruction was far more likely to get a result than simply shouting "no" – a fact she wished she'd known from day one of dog ownership.

She shouted it again, and Kali stopped, and slowly lowered herself to the floor, but her hair was standing up along her back. Anyone who said that a dog couldn't be tense while they were in a "down" position had not seen a revved-up Rottie. Her ears were pricked, her forehead was furrowed, and her breath was coming in sharp pants as she rolled her eyes, showing the whites.

Penny got to her feet and brushed the dry leaves and grass from her knees as she moved slowly and calmly towards Kali, approaching from the side. She murmured a stream of "good girl, stay there, what a good girl" as she worked her way to Kali.

Kali glanced up at her. Her fur was lying smooth again, and though Penny didn't like to assign human emotions to the dog, she did appear somewhat sheepish.

"What set you off?" Penny said, trying not to sound cross. She peered into the bushes.

Nothing. Nothing but a white carrier bag, caught on some twigs. Penny walked into the undergrowth and pulled it free, balling it up so she could take it home and dispose of it properly.

"It was a carrier bag. What did you think it was?" Penny said to Kali.

Kali licked her lips and looked away.

"Oh, daft thing. It's all right," Penny said, and knelt beside her to give her a reassuring fuss. Kali rolled, stiff-legged, onto her side, presenting her belly for a rub. All was forgiven.

Penny pushed the rubbish into a side pocket on her

rucksack and then sat on it again. She was still thinking about Mandy, and the paintings that Alec had done of her.

Mandy, who twenty years ago had looked like Francine did now.

Francine, who had gone to see Alec but he hadn't answered the door.

Alec, who was quite possibly not entirely stable in his mind, living in a lonely spot and avoiding company.

Penny tried to picture those events in her head. Francine went to see Alec on Thursday night. Had he thought it was Mandy? Had it triggered some strange flashback? Certainly, on Friday, Alec had gone to see Reg and that's when he'd asked to track "Amanda Fredericks" down, not knowing that she had changed back to her maiden name. And then he'd spoken with Carl, and Carl had given Alec the contact details for Mandy.

And Mandy had confessed, eventually, that she and Alec had met up.

He would have seen, by then, that Mandy was much changed. He would have known, by then, that Francine's visit was nothing to do with Mandy or the past.

Reactions, Penny thought, opening her eyes and staring

directly at the now-slumbering dog. *We react on what we see, viscerally, without thought or logic, don't we? I wonder if Alec had reacted like that, prompting a night of painting and art, going over the past, the court case, Mandy and Carl.*

Had Alec and Mandy had an affair?

Yet Alec's evidence had convicted Mandy.

Penny got up and undid her bag, fishing around until she could pull out a flapjack and a banana. She sat back down, on the grass this time, her legs straight out in front of her. Kali wandered over and flopped down with a groan and a sigh, leaning along Penny's legs.

Mandy had confessed to gambling. Had she taken part in the robbery to pay her gambling debts?

Something was still not adding up.

Mandy seemed like a "normal" woman. How *did* such an average woman end up being part of a criminal gang?

* * * *

Penny slept surprisingly well. The tent didn't collapse, she didn't freeze to death, and she found the perfect spot to use Drew's trowel.

She woke too early as the birds ramped up with an incredibly noisy dawn chorus and the sun made the inside of the tent into a furnace very quickly.

Kali was lying at the entrance to the tent, in the small porch area, her head poking out under the flap so that Penny could only see her body and wagging tail. Penny reached over, still sitting in her sleeping bag, and unzipped the tent fully. Kali simply rolled out onto the grass.

Penny had packed cold food for her own breakfast and Kali's usual dry kibble. They ate sitting together, and Penny felt calmer, but no closer to the answer of who killed Alec Goodwin.

What did the others think? She knew, from her last conversation with Francine, that she still thought Barry might be the culprit, although she no longer thought Steve was in on the act. Steve was a golden boy for her, now, which in itself made Penny suspicious of him. Penny thought he was responsible for trashing the Sculpture Trail, in a fit of anger.

Penny's heart pulled her back to Mandy, or Carl.

Or Mandy and Carl.

For both had lied.

She sighed. "Time to pack up and head home, Kali."

Who knows, she thought. *Maybe it would have all changed while I was out here. And there's a week until the Summer Fair and the grand opening of the Sculpture Trail. Maybe my time would be better spent in helping Francine and Ginni, not pointlessly pursing this case.*

She stopped as she was pulling up a tent peg.

If I don't pursue it, the police will eventually drop it, and who will be mourning poor Alec Goodwin?

I have to continue.

It felt like she'd just committed to pushing a boulder up an endless hill for the rest of her life.

Chapter Twenty-one

Francine was out when Penny got back to the cottage. Because of her early start camping, it was not yet ten o'clock but she was ravenously hungry. Her belly was trying to tell her it was lunchtime already.

Penny went out to the garden, trying to distract herself by drawing some flowers. She'g got no further than sketching out a few broad leaves when her mobile phone rang. It was Ariadne; Penny had stored the number when her sister had called the previous time and she hadn't recognised it.

"Hi!" Penny said happily as she answered.

Ariadne did not sound quite so happy.

"What did you send me flowers for?"

"Er … to say hi. And I kind of got the impression you might be going through a bit of a bad time," Penny said.

"They were to cheer you up."

"A bad time? You have no idea. What use are flowers to someone having a bad time?"

"They look nice."

Ariadne swore under her breath. "You must have really nice, simple bad times if they can be changed with a pretty bunch of flowers."

Penny had little patience for her sister's spite. She never had. She snapped. "Right, okay, I won't send you flowers again. Got it. Did you ring me up to tell me how bad an idea it was? Or have you anything else to tell me?"

"Like what?"

Penny rolled her eyes to the heavens. "Well, I don't know, do I? Or else I would not be asking." *Aargh.* She made a face at Kali, who ignored her.

There was a silence on the other end of the line. Penny waited.

And waited.

Eventually, she said, in a much softer tone, "Ariadne, you're crying. I can hear you. I am so sorry. Is there anything I can do?"

"Like what?"

Oh, don't let's start this up again. "Seriously," Penny said. "Anything. You have my number and my address, now, from the delivery card. I know we ... I know *I* haven't always been the best sister, and I am sorry. Can I help you? I have some spare money."

"I don't think it's a question of money."

"Is it the kids? Are they all right?"

"You know what the problem is," Ariadne said bitterly. "You always knew. And my goodness, you let me know that you knew."

"It's Owen, isn't it?"

Ariadne snorted but it became a muffled sob once more. "Penny... I don't know what to do."

Penny felt a lump in her throat at the sound of her sister's raw pain. "Ariadne, you must do whatever it takes to keep you and your children safe. Look after yourself so that you can look after them. Do what is right."

"It's not easy."

"The right thing never is," Penny said with feeling. "But keep yourselves *safe*. Please. I've seen too much ... trouble ... lately. Life is short, Ariadne."

"Feels long right now," Ariadne said.

And then the line went dead.

* * * *

It was the first of August. The past few days had passed in a blur, with Francine mostly absent and Penny fulfilling orders from her website.

Now she was standing outside the Community Hall, which had been decked out in red, white and blue.

"The bunting was left over from the VE Day commemorations that we had," Agatha confessed to Penny. They were loitering on the car parking area to the side of the hall, watching the general to and fro.

"It looks good," Penny said. "So is this summer fete an annual thing? I have to say, you know, the turn-out isn't great, is it?"

"It's the summer holidays," Agatha said. "A lot of folks have gone away with their kids, eh? But every single year, the town council try to put on a fete, and every single year, not much happens. You wait until Christmas though. Now, that is a good show!"

"Here he comes." Penny waved and Drew held two

burgers aloft as he came towards them.

"Hi, Agatha! How are you? Would you like a burger?"

"No, no, no, thank you."

Drew passed one to Penny. Agatha made her polite excuses and wandered off. Drew perched on the low wall between the car park and the pavement. "Cheer up," he said. "It's sunny, and you have food. What more could you want?"

"It's so simple for men, isn't it?"

"That's proper sexist, that is," he admonished her.

"Sorry. It's simple for *you*, then."

Drew nodded. "I suppose it is. And why not, though? Life doesn't have to be all complicated."

Penny laughed. Drew really was that simple and straightforward. She raised the half-eaten burger to him in an off-hand toast. "You are right." She couldn't stifle her following sigh, though. "But what a shame we haven't avenged Alec Goodwin."

"*Avenged!* Wow, that sounds heavy. I think you have to have a sword to do some proper avenging."

"It is how I see it," Penny said. "I know he wasn't well-liked but he was *someone*, you know? A human being.

We're all flawed. And everyone deserves justice."

"They are going to call this the 'Alec Goodwin Sculpture Trail'," Drew said. "Everyone agreed to that."

"I know, and that's nice, I suppose."

"Come on. Have you done with your burger? Let's go and look at the first pole."

Penny balled up the wrapper and passed it to Drew to throw into a bin. "Lead on."

* * * *

"How many were completed in the end?" Penny asked.

"All twelve," Drew replied. "What do you think?"

"Amazing."

There was a small crowd around the wooden pole. It was about five feet tall, and rounded like a fence post. It stood on the opposite side of the road to the community hall, and attached to the top part of the pole was a curved piece of aluminium with a relief pattern on it. There were figures, young and old, holding hands.

"This is the first one," Drew said, "and it shows the ethos behind the Community Hall."

302

"Great. But how will visitors know what it is about, and how to find the next one?"

"They are having some information boards made up, with braille and everything. I can't believe we got all our poles done, and they haven't managed to get the boards finished. There will be maps printed as well, and leaflets."

"So these poles go all around Glenfield?"

"Yes. The next one is in the open market area. Shall we go and see?"

Drew and Penny walked along Back Street and between Alf's Garage and the covered market, turning left along the High Street towards the open market. She could see the pole from quite a distance, as the sun shone and reflected off the aluminium. There were a handful of people looking at it, including Steve.

"Hey, Steve, how's it going?" Drew said cheerily.

Steve actually smiled back, and Penny grinned. The sullen young man had a hint of pride on his face. "Yeah, all right," he said gruffly. "Now then, Penny."

"I love these," she said, without hesitation. "Well done, Steve, and you too, Drew."

"Nah, it were my aunt and your mate Francine," Steve

said.

"You too," Penny said. "You have been amazing." She wanted to say more, to tell him he was brave and maturing and generally wonderful, but she bit it back. He would have died of embarrassment in front of strangers and friends alike.

"Yeah, well, thanks," he muttered, and tried to hide his smile, but she knew it was enough.

"Now what for you?" she asked. "This will look good on job applications, won't it?"

"Maybe, yeah." He stepped back, and she followed his lead, drawing away from the others. "Penny, uh, thanks and all that, for not being all … judgemental. You know, about my studies and stuff."

"It's okay. It's not my place to judge. It's really not the end of the world, you know."

"It felt like it to me," he said, forcefully. He glanced up and met her gaze briefly, but looked away. "Cos you, and everyone, all think I was kicked out for being a bit rubbish, don't you?"

She'd assumed he had been asked to leave because of missing classes or something similar, or maybe some violent outbursts in a lecture. She didn't say that. She simply asked, "Why didn't you finish, Steve?"

"I messed up a lot in my second year," he said. "I were drinking and partying and being a student, you know? And yeah, so I missed a load of essays and that. And they called me in and had a right go at me."

She nodded. "And you pulled yourself together?"

"Yeah. I did. Cos I really, really wanted my degree. I wanted to prove I could do it."

"To your family?"

"To me," he said fiercely. "To *me*. And I was nearly there, and all. I really was. But then some … lowlife … nicked my dissertation." He added a few colourful swearwords, and Penny understood, and didn't get offended.

"Did they submit it as their own?"

"Yeah, they did, and the thing was, they were some golden student all the time, so when it came to the investigation, who got done for it? Yeah, me."

"Surely there was evidence. Proof, in your notes and everything."

"You'd think so. Thing is, right, my English isn't the best. I struggle with my spelling. Not as bad as Barry, you know. He can sign his name and that's about it, did you know that? He went to that special school. But he has turned out okay. Anyway. So my notes were a mess, and my first draft was a mess, but when Archie stole my work, he had it properly edited and tidied up. So his essay was like a really, really good version of mine. And they believed him over me, because I had a bad history. But all the while, I was innocent."

"Oh, Steve, that is awful! I feel sick on your behalf. Surely something can be done…" Penny was already writing strong letters in her head.

"No, no. It's kinda all right now. I mean, no, it isn't, but I'm moving on, like what you told me and all."

"I wouldn't be so forgiving."

He shrugged. "I can waste a lot of time getting angry," he said, "or I can do sommat else with my life. I dunno what, yet, but I'm going to work for Aunt Ginni and look at what college courses are starting up this autumn."

"Blacksmithing!" Drew said, interrupting them. He appeared between them and flung his arms around both their shoulders, pulling them in close.

"No, gerroff me," Steve said, pushing him away, and

grinning, and laughing.

* * * *

Penny left Drew with Steve and walked back to the community hall. Francine was supervising a stall there, and she had promised to keep her company.

She walked slowly.

Steve's words and his unfortunate situation played in her mind. She felt dreadful for him, and wished he would take on the university and fight the unfairness. But that was his fight, not hers. She had to stay out of it.

He was innocent, he was innocent, her brain chanted at her.

And then it hit her.

What if Mandy had been innocent of that crime, all those years ago?

On whose evidence was she convicted?

Alec's.

But what if ... like the university ... Alec had been misled? Not by anyone but his own self and his arrogant confidence in his artistic abilities to recognise and remember a face?

Mandy had said she forgave Alec. She said she'd moved

on. That made more sense if she had been innocent.

And if she had done ten years for a crime she had not committed, and had somehow found it within herself to move on from that … *wow*, thought Penny. *She's a bigger person than I could ever be. I'd have been furious, for the rest of my natural life.*

Like I am angry on Steve's behalf.

Then she stopped dead on the pavement. *What about Carl, her husband?*

Had he known that Mandy was innocent, and that Alec had – accidentally or wilfully – been instrumental in convicting the wrong person? If Carl had known that Mandy was innocent, he would have had every right to want to visit vengeance upon his former best friend.

And if he had found out … when had he found out?

Penny started walking again, very quickly, and she pulled out her mobile phone to dial Cath as she went.

* * * *

"Ginni had poet's narcissus in her shop," Cath said. "The evidence doesn't just point to Carl alone." She had been at home when Penny rang, and now she was standing in the Community Hall with Penny and Francine. Most people were outside, milling around the burger van.

"Ginni has very little motive," Penny insisted. "Either on her own part, or on Steve's behalf."

"There's more. Barry also had the chance to obtain the poison," Cath said. "He works for various agencies and gangs, doing piecework in factories and fields."

"Barry has no motive!"

"Apart from the fact that he was being evicted and he couldn't read properly so he couldn't fight the eviction."

"He had plenty of people on his side, helping him," Penny pointed out. "I met one of his neighbours. That's why the eviction was taking so long. You can't just throw people out of their houses."

"Hmm. Right, so you're saying that Alec was mistaken when he gave evidence to the court?"

"Yes. He had heard the description of the accomplice in the jewellery heist, and it matched Mandy. But as we know, people can look similar. Even you can see that Mandy, twenty years ago, looked like Francine does now."

Cath nodded. "Yes, I can see that. And the van that was seen there?"

"The white van was filthy with red dust from the Fens. It can't have been Ginni's. She keeps it spotless. Carl has a white van and he lives out on the Fens."

Cath rolled her eyes. "Today is my day off. I had plans, you know? Plans that involved moving between the sofa and the fridge. I have packed my husband and the kids off to a swimming pool party and we were going to the cinema later this afternoon." She sighed. "Right. Come on with me up to the station. If we get this over with, I might still make it to the film, and be a normal mother."

"Normal?" Penny said, laughing.

"Shut up. Let's go."

CHAPTER TWENTY-TWO

Francine abandoned her stall in the Community Hall. "It will be fine. Who would want to steal some leaflets and a display about the project?" she asked as she followed Cath and Penny into the police station.

"You'd be amazed," Cath said. "Thieves took the lead from the roof of Wanstead Police Station, you know."

"That is class."

"That is *crime*," said the dour desk sergeant who was in his permanent place behind the plastic screen.

"Do you have a twin?" Penny asked.

"No. I just loathe my wife and prefer to work."

"I have met your wife and she is delightful," Cath said sharply. "And you don't deserve her. Is Inspector Travis about?"

"He is. He got your call, and went to fill himself with

coffee. He said he was going to need it. Interview room six. Go on through."

Interview room six was empty. Penny and Francine were left alone while Cath went off in search of Inspector Travis, and at first they filled the time by talking about the Sculpture Trail.

Then silence fell. Penny watched Francine carefully. She was pacing around, twisting her hands together. Eventually Penny said, "Now, I'm only just opening up to reading other people's body language, but is something on your mind, Francine?"

"Um, yeah. I think it's time I moved out. I know I mentioned it before. Well, I'm ready to go now."

Penny blinked. Her heart thumped, and she felt a little odd.

This was good news, right?

"Oh. I see. Where are you going?"

"Are you okay with this?" Francine said.

"Yes. Yes, of course I am! You must do what you feel best ... why do I feel like we're having a really difficult conversation about something that should be easy?"

Francine smiled sheepishly. "I know you struggled

312

when I turned up and didn't leave. I really needed the space and I am so grateful to you. I didn't mean to stay so long, but when you needed me …"

"I needed you?"

"You did."

Penny sighed, and she was still feeling funny. "I think I did. Thank you. But it's okay. It is time to move on."

"I've got something to tell you, though. Before I go. Please don't be mad at me. You can't blame me any more than I blame myself…"

Now Penny's odd feeling turned her belly to water. "What have you done?"

"I was trying to look after Kali. I wanted to have fun with her. I wanted her to like me."

"She does!"

"I wanted to give her treats. And I think that is what made her ill. She wasn't poisoned by anyone. Except me."

Penny's palms were slippery with sweat and she felt hot. She reminded herself that Kali had recovered and was doing fine. "What on earth did you feed her?"

"A chocolate bar."

"You stupid–" Penny rolled her eyes to the ceiling and

bit her own tongue. *Deep breaths, Penny. There was no lasting harm.* "Oh, Francine. You can't give chocolate to a dog."

"I know that … now."

Penny sighed. "Come here."

"Why?"

"For a hug. You look like you need one."

"But I…"

"You do. Come here." Penny advanced upon Francine and grabbed her. "It was a mistake. I could never, ever believe that you would cause harm to Kali, or any living creature. Thank you for being honest."

Penny squeezed Francine for a few long seconds before releasing her. "And now, tell me where you're going. Because I am going to miss you, you know."

"I'm not going far," Francine said. "In fact, I'm in negotiations to buy Alec Goodwin's house. I've had an offer on my London place; the tenants that I let it to want to buy it. I'm staying in Upper Glenfield."

"Wow," Penny said, followed by, "Oh no. I just can't get rid of you, can I?"

"The universe wills it."

"The universe has got it in for me," Cath grumbled,

entering suddenly, followed by Inspector Travis. "I was supposed to be at home right now."

There was a flurry of introductions between the beetle-browed Inspector, and Francine, who pinked and smiled and nearly curtseyed.

"Sorry about the delay, ladies," Inspector Travis said. Penny loathed being called a lady, for reasons she was not entirely sure about but if pressed she would have said "feminism." Francine, on the other hand, delighted in the reference.

"It's quite all right!" Francine said. "Your job is very important. You people don't get enough recognition."

Penny smiled. If being called a lady was bad, "you people" was probably worse.

Inspector Travis held Francine's gaze for a second too long, trying to work out if she was being sarcastic. Then he gave a slight shake of his head, and said, "Well, quite. Thank you. We've just being talking to Carl Fredericks."

Penny stiffened. "Where is he?" she said, looking around as if he were about to burst through the door.

"Making himself comfortable, as much as he can, in one of our cells for the moment," Cath said.

"Oh my goodness!" Penny blurted out. "Has he confessed? Was I *right?*"

"He wants to talk to you," Inspector Travis said. "I would suggest that this is unwise, and I told him so, but he was insistent. I had to I promise him I'd come to tell you. And I already know what you're going to say."

"Of course I'll talk with him!" Penny said. "Oh, wait … not alone, right? I don't think I want to be alone with him."

"Definitely not," Inspector Travis said. "Okay. I suppose all four of us, and him … we're going to need more chairs. Cath, if you could …"

"I'm on it."

* * * *

Carl Fredericks shuffled into the interview room, flanked by a uniformed officer who nodded to Inspector Travis, and quickly disappeared. He was wearing a plaid shirt and jeans, and wasn't cuffed.

Cath was messing around with a recording machine that sat on the desk.

"You still use tapes?" Penny said. "That's retro, that is."

"We've got quite a stock to get through," Cath said. "And it's simple technology. A lot of forces are going digital, and I suppose we will, in the end. But for now ... yes, we're old school."

Penny was feeling quite excited until Cath said, "Anyway, I'm just getting this ready for the formal interview later. You won't be here for that. Sorry."

"Oh."

Carl glared at Penny. "Yeah, but no doubt you lot will tell this meddling idiot everything."

"No," Inspector Travis said. "Now, this is all contrary to our usual protocols; Carl, this is instead of your phone call. We're making a concession. You can rest assured, however, that whatever you tell us – in the formal interview later – will remain part of police investigations and Ms May will only know what is allowed to be in the public domain."

Carl spluttered with indignation. "Ar, but this is Lincolnshire, so *everything* is in the public domain. You can't sneeze without your neighbours knowing and making up some tale about it."

"Mr Fredericks," Penny said, folding her arms. "You have asked to talk with me. I'm sorry if you feel I have been meddling. I simply take an interest in community matters."

He rolled his eyes at her. "Hark at you."

"We know you killed Alec," she said, ignoring Inspector Travis's warning hiss. "I am simply curious as to why you did it."

Carl shrugged and stayed quiet.

Penny started to tick the evidence off on her fingers. "Look, your dirty van was seen there. Your business handles exactly the type of plant that poisoned him. You knew how he lived so you must have visited him. You knew he was reclusive and not involved in the community."

"Ar, so what? Why would I have wanted to do him in?"

"Mr Fredericks, did you know that your ex-wife was innocent when she was convicted of a part in that jewellery heist?"

Carl's eyes closed in a slow blink. "She was found guilty," he said.

"Yes, but she wasn't guilty, was she?"

"I thought she was, at the time. Alec had recognised

318

her from the description in the court case when he was working as an artist."

Cath interrupted. "That's not enough to convict anyone."

Carl looked sad. "It is when that person also has a large sum of money in her possession that she can't account for, especially when she'd had her hours cut at work. Which I didn't know about at the time, I might add."

"That her hours had been cut?"

"Ar, that. She lied to me. She said she were still working full time. But she weren't. Thing is … she had a bit of an issue with gambling, did our Mandy."

Penny nodded. "We know. She told us."

"Ah, did she?" He looked a little relieved. "Right. Okay, then. So she won big, but she didn't want to tell me where she'd got the money from. Obviously once she'd been arrested, she tried to say, but she weren't believed because there was no record. She'd been going to Skegness and all over, to dodgy betting shops. This was before you could gamble away on the internet at home. She were going to places that didn't even have cctv or decent records. So she couldn't prove nothing, and I didn't believe her, and she were sent down."

"But did *Alec* know she was innocent? Did he do this deliberately?" Penny asked.

At the mention of Alec's name, Carl's sad expression faded into one of anger, his brows lowering and his jaw becoming tight. "Ar. Nah. Maybe. He reckoned that he didn't know she were innocent at first. He said he would never have given evidence. But when he did find out he never, ever retracted his statement. Thing is, that Alec Goodwin were a first class coward. Why do you think he lived out there on his own? Why do you think he never spoke to no one? Coward. He just couldn't handle life."

"But he was your friend…"

"Was. He had been. But I had no time for him once I knew what he'd done, and nothing he could say would change that. Mandy … she were stupid for forgiving him."

"You tried to frame her for the murder!"

"No, no, no," Carl said, shaking his head. He rubbed his hand over his face, and his voice was muffled. "I didn't want to. I just wanted to get you guys off my back. You were closing in. And she were stupid, really, she were. She shouldn't have forgiven him. She shouldn't have met up with him. He ruined it all, between us, our life, her life, everything. He had to pay."

Carl was choking back sobs now, and Penny felt a pang of sympathy as she watched him unravel in front of her. He kept rubbing at his eyes, and coughing. "Alec were a snob, a coward and a snob, and he didn't deserve the nice things he had, and he didn't deserve her forgiveness, and he definitely didn't deserve to enjoy the things that he did."

"Like posh coffee."

"None of it," Carl said huskily. "He deserved only to die."

With that bald statement, Penny's sympathy faded abruptly and she turned to Cath and Inspector Travis.

She didn't need to say anything. Cath led Penny and Francine out of the interview room and back along the corridor to the public reception area.

They stood for a moment in silence. Penny ran it all through her mind again. She wished she could have asked *how* it had all happened, but she knew she'd have to wait for the official reports. Instead, she said, "Cath, why do you think Alec didn't stand up for Mandy once he knew she'd been wrongfully convicted?"

"He would have lost his job, and possibly gone to jail himself."

"My goodness," Penny said. "The lengths people go to just to keep their jobs."

Cath frowned. "Jobs are not so easy to come by that most people can throw them away," she said sternly.

"Ouch. Yes, you are totally right. I'm sorry. I am a crass idiot."

Francine threw her arm around Penny and hugged her. "It's okay," she said, soothingly. "You're *our* crass idiot. Come on. Shall we go grab some food?"

"Are you paying?"

"A burger it is, then."

CHAPTER TWENTY-THREE

The cottage was empty.

Well, not quite. Penny and Kali sat in the front room, at either end of the sofa, each submerged in their own thoughts. Penny was thinking about how quiet it was, without Francine. Kali was probably thinking about food.

It was two weeks since Carl Fredericks had confessed to murdering Alec Goodwin, and one week since Francine had moved out. She wasn't yet able to move into the house that she was buying; the wheels of probate turned very slowly and Alec's estate was still being unravelled by the solicitors. Penny wondered if the sale would fall through. Nothing, yet, was certain.

But Francine was hopeful, and for Francine, hope was a bright and perfect thing.

The universe would sort it out, Francine had told

Penny. Things will happen as they happen.

Not if you don't make them happen, Penny thought. *But Francine is happy, and so I am happy.*

It was going to take a while to get used to the peace of her space once more. Francine had taken a short-term let in a flat in Lincoln. She told Penny that she had encroached on her good nature for long enough, and now it was time to stand on her own two feet.

Penny wondered how much this had to do with the twinkle in the eye of Inspector Travis. But she kept her suspicions to herself, this time.

Francine had pre-emptively been to visit Barry, and assured him that he would be able to continue renting his shack. She also promised to do some maintenance on it. Barry seemed happy.

She also spoke of taking in a lodger. Penny wondered if Steve would go for it, at least while he got himself back on track. Privately she hoped that Steve would get up and go – travel the world, work in a bar in Australia, sleep on a beach in Bangkok – but he probably wouldn't. He was rooted in Glenfield.

Again, she kept her advice to herself.

The culprit who had trashed the Sculpture Trail had never owned up, but she felt, in her gut, it had been Steve. She saw no reason to pursue it.

Perhaps, like Mandy Jones – Amanda Fredericks – she, too, was learning to move on from things.

The details of the murder of Alec had emerged in the press, with gaps that Penny was able to fill in from her own knowledge and guesswork.

The newspapers had said that Carl had gone to see Alec, taking a gift of fine coffee, into which he had ground a large amount of poet's narcissus bulb. The bitter taste of the alkaloid had been disguised by the coffee.

The papers hadn't explained why Carl had suddenly been compelled to visit Alec and wreak his vengeance on him. Penny could piece it together, though.

Francine had gone to see Alec the day before he was killed. Alec had seen her peering through the glass, and hidden from her. That was a fact.

What happened then, Penny could only guess at. He had a fresh artwork on his easel and he had painted a woman that looked like Francine – but it was Mandy, from his past. The woman he'd sent to prison, and about whom he had been too cowardly to confess his perjury. It seemed to Penny that he had spent the night in a painting frenzy, unsettled by the sight of the woman who looked like Mandy.

The next day, still unsettled, and probably suffering from lack of sleep, he had called Carl, wanting to talk to Mandy. Carl had warned Mandy about it. Mandy, however, had fought and faced her demons, and told Carl that "Alec was forgiven" and more than that – she'd gone to meet him.

Carl's fury at Mandy's apparent acquiescence had been revealed in the day in the police station, and Penny knew that this was his trigger to seek Alec out, and destroy him.

Carl and Alec. Penny shook her head. Both men were damaged and stuck in their pasts, and couldn't move forward. Mandy had been the sanest one among them, and Penny had a deep respect for the woman. She didn't think she could have been so serene in her position.

But then, as even Steve said about his disastrous university career – what good would stressing and gnawing about it really do?

She was glad that it was wrapped up, and glad that Mandy had finally cleared her name. She hoped that she had kept her job in the shop, and was happy in her little flat. She seemed to be doing good for others in the gambling support society, and her life had meaning.

As for Carl, he'd serve his time. Penny wondered if he would endure as serenely as Mandy. She suspected not.

Penny glanced at her watch. She had a date with Drew that evening, and she was looking forward to it. They were off to the cinema. He had surprised her by suggesting a European arthouse film, and she had felt slightly ashamed of her surprise until he confessed that he had no idea what it was about but had asked Brian Davenport, the manager of the hotel where he ran his field craft courses, what sort of film would impress "a cultured woman from London."

Brian considered himself to be a man with taste, and had provided a string of recommendations.

Kali yawned and stretched and tipped her head back, peeking at Penny from the corner of her eyes. It wasn't quite time to feed her yet, but Kali liked to be prepared and ready.

Dogs were always ready for food.

Penny felt a little bereft. The Sculpture Trail was done. The case was over. She had her art and craft work to get on with. She had had so many plans that had fallen to one side, and now she didn't have much motivation to pick up where she had left off. She'd promised Lee that she would return to the urban exploration group, and bring Drew. She'd vaguely agreed to go to a few more craft fairs with Mary, though she didn't want to face a small minority of unfriendly makers. She was still volunteering at the weekend for the dogs' home, but that was one afternoon a week.

I need a plan, an aim, a purpose, she decided. Retirement didn't mean stultification, especially when it was early retirement.

It had to be something with meaning, she thought. Yeah, she could learn furniture restoration or some-such, but it had to have meaning for her.

Maybe she should take a leaf out of Francine's book, and simply wait for the universe to show her what her next move ought to be. If she let herself be open to signs, as Francine urged, something would turn up.

Penny glanced to the door, expecting the universe to oblige immediately. No one knocked.

She laughed at herself, sighed, and dropped her half-drunk cup of tea when there was a sudden explosion of furious knocking.

Kali leaped to the floor, the solid mug bounced and rolled on the carpet, and tea soaked straight into the rug.

The knocking continued.

Penny sent Kali to her mat with a stern word, and went to see what the universe had brought.

Ariadne.

And two of her three children.

And a facial expression of dire foreboding...

The End

Author's Afterword

This is the bit you don't need to read, but if you enjoyed the book you might want to find out more.

I've got a website at http://www.issybrooke.com where I have more information about the characters, about Lincolnshire, and the fictional town of Glenfield - including a map.

The dog in this story, Kali, is based on our own rescue dog, a Rottie cross called Stella. That's her on the cover of this book. She's a stressed out and reactive thing, and we're still working through her issues. I wish it was as easy as Penny found it … you can read more about dogs on my website, too. And look at photos. Everyone loves photos of dogs, right?

I'm on Facebook:
https://www.facebook.com/issy.brooke – and Twitter here – @IssyBrooke – but as for the million other social media sites, nope. I'd rather be writing…

Thank you for reading.

Issy.

Made in United States
North Haven, CT
22 March 2023

34390920R00200